WE HAVE SEEN THE BEST OF OUR TIMES

FOR MY MOTHER

WE HAVE SEEN THE BEST OF OUR TIMES

Short Stories by

Nancy A. J. Potter

ALFRED · A · KNOPF · *New York* · 1968

SOME OF THE STORIES IN THIS COLLECTION HAVE BEEN PRINTED IN THE FOLLOWING MAGAZINES:

The Kenyon Review "WE HAVE SEEN THE BEST OF OUR TIMES,"
"DIVORCING THE DEAD HUSBAND"
The Colorado Quarterly "THE CROOKED MAN," "THE COLLECTION"
Shenandoah "JUST TELL ME ALL YOUR TROUBLES"
The Massachusetts Review "THE HAPPIEST YOU'VE EVER BEEN"
Prairie Schooner "IN UNION SWEET"
Four Quarters "SUNDAY'S CHILDREN"
Noetics "THE SAVED MAN"
Copyright © 1964 by The Fugitive Press

CONTENTS

We have seen the best of our times

WE HAVE SEEN
THE BEST OF
OUR TIMES

◆§◊ Dillworth Plante
was a gray man even in what youth he had. His mother
remembered that he had cried so little and slept so stonily
as a baby that people passing his carriage often thought him
dead. Once, when Mrs. Plante came out of Haskel and
Porteus (where she had been buying a new lace insertion for
the plum-colored crepe dress she wore for best from 1901 until
1914), she found an utter stranger bending over Dillworth's
wicker carriage. Mrs. Plante's mind operated as a series of
pictures, always negative and cautionary. At that second she
saw gypsies and New York gangsters and procurers for pick-
pocket rings of children, but the face over the carriage bonnet
was compassionate and frozen into O's of wonder. "Your
baby's alive! I thought the poor little tyke was dead."

The Plantes had risen painfully into respectability, and
Dillworth was the worn-out result. In those illustrated re-

gional biographical dictionaries of the 1890's for which salesmen sold space, $10 a half-column, $50 a whole page, the Plantes bought two pages, one for the family tree and the other for a photograph of Reverend Ezra Plante, his black signature reproduced below. Ezra was WCTU chaplain; after losing his faith, he coughed and cleared his throat during the sermons so that it was hard to know their drift. His congregation was more worried about fellowship than faith, anyway. Ezra's son, Sam Plante (Dillworth's father), went away to the Payne Business College in Omaha and learned Morse code, Pitman shorthand, double-ledger bookkeeping, and how to fasten a handkerchief under his sleeve elastic, one corner peeping over the wrist, ready to be pulled out. He coughed too. But did not have to give sermons, because he became paymaster for the Reynolds Bicycle Works in Grand Island. His wife, Dillworth's mother, saved money by serving dried beef or codfish or beans and by not going anywhere for which the plum dress was not satisfactory. Their house was cold and thin. The inside smelled of bacon and of burned starch from the shirts Mrs. Plante did—two a day. Sam came home for lunch and a fresh shirt.

Dillworth wore brown corduroy knickers and fresh shirts and practiced the piano with stub-fingered violence and a built-in metronome. He liked recitals and soon was the biggest boy those July evenings when the girls' organdy skirts rose stickily from the piano bench. He bowed low before the mothers and then sat down to "May Night," "Finlandia," and the "Schönbrunner Walzer" as encore. It was too bad his nervous teeth left bloody hangnails, but no one was close enough to the stage to see them.

As the oldest male pupil, he introduced the two-hour recital program, speaking in short, jerky sentences. One year,
when Lucy-Mae and Marilyn-Jo Belcher, dressed as daffodils,
did an interpretive dance while their older sister, Odell, played
the "Waltz of the Flowers," he fixed the lights which shifted
red, green, and yellow spots over them.

·   ·   ·

Nettie Reynolds
the piano teacher gave the music lessons in the front parlor
of her late father, the bicycle-maker. The mantel of the
bricked-in fireplace was a kind of trophy case for her: little
vases and bowls and fans and wind-up animals given at
Christmas by pupils, the gifts they had wanted for themselves
but she kept; a set of great masters of the piano cut from
Ivory soap; and the best Christmas cards—left there until
they were replaced by summer post cards of the Black Hills
or the Omaha Stockyards. After the recital at the end of June
there was a picnic: punch and cake in the grape arbor.

The thinnest parts of Nettie Reynolds, then in her indefi-
nite twenties, were her wrists and ankles. She could circle
her wrist with her thumb and index finger, and did this frequently. Her hair was thin too. Otherwise, she was a series
of mounds and curved surfaces, unknown to sunlight or human sight. Except for her hands, she seemed to have no bones,
but only deeply buried blue veins.

"Now," she would say to eleven-year-old Dillworth
Plante, fumbling at his music roll, "we will try the Rimski-
Korsakov," and she would flick back the shawl that covered
the Steinway when it was at rest. And so he would begin far

away the "Caucasian March": thum-thum-thumpa-thumpa, sinking, coming closer, little dark men on stocky horses, with a great bush of hair under their noses like Rimski-Korsakov, bandmaster, hollow-cheeked under his astrakhan cap, who peered from the left side of the page of Schirmer's fourth-year Music Library for American Students. The Caucasians came nearer, almost into the parlor, thumpa, thumpa. "Less pedal!" Miss Reynolds cried.

He especially admired the way she flipped the shawl back, holding it between the tip of her thumb and middle finger. While he played, she kept her right hand in the black island at the end of the ivory keys. Her left hand crouched politely in her lap as if she were sitting at a dinner table. In later years no one who had taken lessons from her could remember what she looked like. Only fierce piano teachers who shout and stamp and hit fingers are remembered. Nettie's thin, blue-veined hand rested on its white handkerchief on the black shelter. Already she had decided to have a matronly figure, which meant a slow-rising bosom which sloped finally toward her knees, uninterrupted by waist. Dillworth at eleven had not noticed except to approve her similarity to his mother. She looked straight at the name Steinway and beneath that at his hands. He had begun to wear a diamond ring pronged into very yellow gold. It was a pinky ring, but he wore it now on his third finger.

When Dillworth was fifteen, Mrs. Plante decided it would be nice if he learned to play the trumpet. He went Saturdays to the basement of a German bandmaster who didn't know what to do with anyone who took the trumpet so seriously and had so little talent. So he went back to Nettie Reynolds, not on a financial basis, more to keep up his skill.

•   •   •

The schools, elementary and secondary, that Dillworth Plante attended left him bloodless and untried. When he had finished twelfth grade—the year the Great War was over—it was as if his teachers had forgotten to transplant him in time. Although they praised him aloud, they knew he was more involved in the ideas behind subjects than in the subjects themselves. Or, at least, so they told themselves, since they did not understand him at all. Before he began French 1, he was so pleased with the image of himself reading another language that the Plantes ordered for him from Marshall Field a deluxe edition of Victor Hugo, printed in Paris. He polished the red buckram spines and cut all the pages and translated exactly the first 300 words of *Les Miserables* (he had counted every word) before he put away the set. In his autograph book one classmate wrote: "His eyes are on the stars." This association with the stars could have been suggested by his enthusiasm for the telescope he was then winning for 100 *Saturday Evening Post* subscriptions. He was fascinated by subjects the school didn't teach—psychology, Hebrew, astronomy.

"When he decides what to throw his resources behind," Horace Cheney, principal, told the Plantes on graduation night, "Dillworth will be a powerhouse, a powerhouse." Cheney's frame shook with the word, and his eyes strained earnestly from their sockets.

"It might be best to let him make up his mind before he goes on," Sam Plante said. He knew how little stability was in the fickle world of commerce.

Mrs. Plante agreed that you shouldn't wear yourself out making false starts; better to know where you would fit and groom yourself for that.

So the other bright boy in the class went to the state college to become a science teacher, and their classmates went back to the farms or on to the sewing-machine factory, while Dillworth groomed himself for the risky game of outwitting the future. Fixing his eyes on the future, he underestimated the width of the foreground and was sharply tripped by the present. Someone else would have laughed and brushed through the resisting cobwebs the future wore, but he took them seriously, was sure that he had to settle everything at home before he could begin the true life and adventures of Dillworth Plante. He was positive they were well worth waiting for.

Meanwhile he played a great holding action with the present. If his aging parents walked slowly, he bought them tonics. If a high-school classmate was rumored to be successful and happily married, he discounted the rumor. If he could have painted the autumn leaves green and stuck them back on the trees, he would have. The effort took so much time and energy that he begrudged the three or four calls a week he had to make on insurance clients. Sam had arranged for him to handle a few inquiry calls for the local agent—just until he decided what to do.

There seemed barely enough time for Dillworth to practice for the Wednesday nights with Nettie Reynolds.

•   •   •

The piano
was a disappointment to both of them. It promised so much
and gave so little. Nature had played a quaint trick on Nettie:
despite her private indifference to music, she had perfect pitch
and timing. Those alone convinced parents, teachers, and
even the director of the Omaha Conservatory of her ultimate
promise as an Artist—they had said the word with awe. But
at the conservatory, listening to concerts made her nervous
and sometimes upset her stomach. It unsettled what confidence she had and seemed to have nothing to do with life.
She preferred silence, and seldom played except as penance
in church and at funerals. When it was necessary to let a
pupil hear how Paderewski had played Chopin, she would
wind the victrola, fit the heavy record to the turntable, thread
the needle to the first groove, and turn the sound knob almost off. It was always a shock for her students to hear some
years later how loudly professional pianists played.

In Dillworth she observed the signs of another music hater.
All the time he played, careful fingers accurately, deliberately
stabbing the keys, his face was drawn toward his pouting
mouth. When it was over, he looked as if weights had been
lifted from his head and arms.

One day he asked: "Does playing ever fill your head with
pressures?"

"All the time," she answered, "until it practically bursts."

"It grows easier to bear, I suppose, as you do more of it?"

"No, it hasn't seemed to," she answered. "Some people,
no matter how much they play, are still uncomfortable with

music. They try every composer and then accompanying other instruments—as if that might make the difference. Then one day they realize the fault is not with the piano but with themselves."

Dillworth could not realize that she was confessing her own experiences, and he kept on searching for the composer or the arrangement that would make the difference. In a houseful of abandoned projects he believed in the discipline of music.

•   •   •

His father
Sam fell dead, used-up and white-faced, on the linoleum one morning, striking his head on the kitchen table, leaving a little mark that Mrs. Plante often stared at later, but could not tell anyone about. "Sam's place," she whispered, stroking it. She had stroked the casket and said, "Sam's little home," at which point Nettie Reynolds surprised everyone by crying —the first and last time anyone ever saw her do it. That was what they remembered afterward about the funeral: Nettie Reynolds crying, playing "Rock of Ages," and crying.

It was possible, if she had thought about it, that Mrs. Plante liked her husband better dead than alive. "The lovely chrysanthemums and snapdragons on the altar this morning are in loving memory of Samuel Plante"; "Mrs. Samuel Plante has ordered a large monument for her late husband in Oak Grove Cemetery. The slab of Carrara marble has been shipped directly from Italy and will be erected under expert supervision this week." That and writing letters to other widows—"You never know how much until they're gone"—she liked most about Sam's death.

His father's dying and Mrs. Plante's widowhood gave Dillworth a new importance, and he began to fill the little house with cheerful announcements about walking to the post office for mail or picking up a case of something or other at freight-office sales. He read all the small print in the A&P ads, and not only could tell what were the best buys in fresh vegetables that week but bought and cooked them. This was so convenient for Mrs. Plante, who had always spent the best part of the morning figuring out how she could cope with dinner, that she sat down at the dining-room table like a delighted guest, which ideal state lasted for seven years until pneumonia carried her off.

.   .   .

The marriage in 1930 of Dillworth (thirty years old) and Nettie (forty-five) was naturally more surprising to them than to anybody else in Grand Island, not only because they were the principals but because they had not expected to marry at all. One day they had gone home to houses they knew like blind men— the rough spot in the plaster of the back stairwell that he had chipped away and eaten as a child, and the broken finger of the Dresden Cupid that she thought she had hidden by turning it to the wall; the next day they offered the place to a total stranger. How could you ever know a person well enough to marry, really? he wondered, but not aloud.

How it happened was, for the changes it wrought, insignificant. Dillworth used to improve on the scene and stretch it out in his mind because it had taken, in reality, almost no time at all. After Mrs. Plante's funeral, Nettie had asked Dillworth for a cold supper. She would have included relatives if they did not all live close enough to drive home, and if she had not been so confused about providing more than Kool-Aid punch and Lorna Doones for one living soul. As it was, she did burn herself quite badly trying to lift the coffee pot from the stove without using the handle. She looked so tired that Dillworth felt sorry for both of them: she so incompetent and he with no one to care for. He reached over and touched her burned hand and asked if he could marry her and come there to live, and she asked: "What will people say?"

They did not say much, because such an old, gray, waistless couple interest only those who know them, not the gaggle of shower-giving girls or bachelor-party boys, and Dillworth and Nettie knew only their families. A certain amount of wonder was expressed in various telephone conversations, and some piano pupils giggled during their lessons the next week, for the milkman had told their mothers about his instructions to stop deliveries at Mr. Plante's and add a quart at Miss Reynolds' every day.

All the time Grand Island did not spend thinking about the wedding, Dillworth speculated about it. He was then in a lonely house which he needed to fill with concerns. Waiting for the mail and shopping for food values, even before his mother's illness, had taken so much time that he had let the Omaha Mutual agent take over his few policies. Their holders were relieved that loyalty to Sam Plante no longer tied them to his abstracted son, upon whom . . . well, could you depend in the hour of need? would you want him around, except to take your mind off accident, death, fire, and horrors? His capacious worry about the future was too personal to include other people; it was as if he would soon be alone in a lovely young world. It was all a matter of being born again, which he was not sure how to accomplish. Possibly he might be launched by some definitive change, and wasn't marriage the greatest of all changes and weren't its effects likely to last longest?

Since he was getting ready for a new and what seemed to be a better life, he arranged for the decent burial of the old. With speed that amazed him as he watched his sprightly self, he divided the clumps of furniture in each room among cousins and helped Salvation Army workers scrape amid the dust for what nobody else wanted. The dim carpets and some jars of preserves in the cellar went to the couple that bought the place, a thin blond couple proud of their first pregnancy —a fact which under other circumstances would have embarrassed him.

Nettie was making no obvious preparations, other than clearing out a couple of bureau drawers and then standing thoughtfully at the kitchen window eating spoonfuls of ginger marmalade directly out of the jar, which she knew Dillworth would never permit again.

One prearranged Sunday afternoon, they were married in a minister's parlor in a town twenty miles north and Dillworth's cousin drove them home. Although Nettie had been careful not to touch the white camellias, they rusted into her blue silk suit. The cousin's wife turned in extravagant politeness from the front seat to stare at them. She was full of irrelevant comparisons.

"The day I married Curtis"—this necessitated a turn and nod toward Curtis, who slouched at the bottom of the thick steering wheel—"it was cold, the flowers froze before they could be delivered, and we had to make crepe-paper ones. The punch like to froze, too. You never saw anything like it." They had not; they had rolled down all the car windows and it was still stifling.

"Curtis and I went to Chicago, and the very first day some thief took eighty dollars right out of his pants pocket. We had to get return trip money from Travelers' Aid."

But Nettie and Dillworth were not going anywhere except back to the neat block of bricks that no one in Grand Island would ever refer to except as the Reynolds place, no matter how long they might be married.

"Curtis and I," the cousin tried again, "hope you'll be as happy as we've been." Despite her staring at him for confirmation, Curtis became so absorbed in steering that he did not seize the hint and add his benediction.

So on that sensible September and Sunday afternoon, they waved from the front door at happy Curtis, still expressionless as he backed carefully out of the crushed-stone driveway, and his wife, whose conspiring smile now included them in the cozy shelter of a Mr. and Mrs. Club.

Dillworth had been holding himself in readiness all day for some urgent signal that the new life was about to begin.

The change might ride in on the grave night wind or fall heavily upon their cramped bodies in the parlor where they were sitting. Some message would come like lightning into this patchy room to sear away their age and commonness and make them lithe figures in some green meadow. But, instead, they sat, each in a soft chair, their voices dying as the dark fell, until finally Dillworth realized they were speaking so low that he had to lean far forward to hear her whispered sentences.

"Father never liked me to put on lights. We used to sit here, quiet like this. You don't mind, do you?"

How could he mind? It was not his house to mind in. Would it, he wondered, become his through usage and service? Or conquest?

"We might as well go upstairs now," she said and he followed her, with the shy step of a prince consort, up the steep stairs and round the hallway to a front bedroom.

· · ·

The bed
had a thin and lumpy mattress, which, of course, Dillworth could not have guessed. It looked soft as sin when he came into the lavender room, dim gold medallions on the wallpaper, everything else lavender: chenille bedspread, dressing-table skirt, possibly the garden scene in a bronze frame (the lavender shade gave such a faint light that you couldn't be sure).

"My momma's bed," Nettie told him. What about her father? Or didn't he? Dillworth wondered.

"You can wash up in the downstairs lavatory," she said.

Patterns spun themselves tight around him. What he did once tonight, he realized, creaking down the stairs, he would always do. Sam and Gertrude Plante had shared an Empire bed, big as a closet. He had never seen them in it, but had crept into the room as a child mornings and turned down the wrinkled sheets until he was satisfied that it was no different from his. This he remembered with comfort as he lathered his hands and squeezed the froth in and out of his palms.

At the lavatory door he waited, listening. On the thin carpet Nettie's slipper stub-toed back, he guessed, toward the lavender bed. He washed his hands again, and his feet, giving her time to get settled. He wished it was morning and they were getting up, and at the same time he wished he had taken the few learning opportunities that when offered had seemed impossible or awkward. A very dark little girl, a relative of the Belchers from St. Louis, had at Marilyn-Jo's wedding reception taken him behind the outbuildings of the Congo Church. He did not realize what she was trying to do until some children with flashlights came running from the church parlor, and then he pushed the little dark girl away.

When he got back to the lavender room, Nettie was in bed, her eyes shut tight, her long thin arms in the short-sleeved gown sticking out of the great mound. He saw again the little bones and the deep veins in her hands and felt those hands stretching his over an octave or correcting the way he held his wrists. Looking at the well-scrubbed face of his old piano teacher made him feel very young and very confident, realizing, as he did, that he would be alive and healthy much longer than she. As he lay down on the surprisingly lumpy bed, he reminded himself that his name would also be on the joint account and on the deed to the house.

·　　　·　　　·

The house

was an absolute square of red brick, three stories worth, with graduated windows. That is, the windows in the attic were quite small, in the second-floor bedrooms they were larger, and you could walk out those on the first floor, had anyone wanted to (Dillworth once thought of it but decided not to), onto a lawn clipped very close. Asher Morgan ran the mower twice over the front lawn, once cross-wise, then up and down, to discourage dandelions before they got ideas. There was a burglar alarm strung around the foundation and Asher had to be careful not to set the thing off. The house had no ex-pression, but sat composed, the lace veils of curtains like lids over its eyes. Arborvitae obscured the front windows and the bedrooms from sun, light, or the seasons. The front door, which no one used, was sheltered by its own portico. Inside, Dillworth took great pleasure in pushing the Bissell sweeper across the Axminster carpets and thinking grand thoughts, while Nettie wandered around touching things. In her wake the lamp-shade tassels and the light-fixture prisms jiggled and the floor boards strained under layers of rug matting.

The old carriage shed had been made over as a garage.

·　　　·　　　·

The car

was a La Salle painted battleship gray. Dillworth rubbed it with a piece of chamois when waiting for the mail every

day (it was the ritual of waiting that mattered, not the results): Sears, Roebuck seasonal catalogs; samples of Daggett
and Ramsdel face cream—Nettie could never resist coupon
offers; bugs identified by the state extension service—Dillworth picked them up and sent them off as a public duty; bro-
chures from steamship lines gaudy with big-smiled and tanned
women in white dresses, leaning over the sides amid the
steamers and confetti. "You could almost live on what you
can pick up free," Dillworth said amid the flotsam that
drifted by—blackhead removers, Christmas card samples,
five fox-trot lessons; maybe not what you wanted *that* morning, but could put aside for sometime.

The car, waiting inside the great carriage-house door and
being stroked by Dillworth Plante, was only taken out after
he had called the weather bureau at Cedar Falls to find out
that it would be a good day. The La Salle's silver nose had
never been poked into fog, rain, hail, or Sunday traffic. The
tight pouches on the doors held flashlights and a copy of the
Automobile Blue Book, Volume T for the trans-continental
tour. Since, however, they were never out after sunset, or past
Kearney, these were as much for show as were the matchbox,
mirror, and lap robe that hung within easy access of the back-
seat passengers that never materialized.

Occasionally, under clear skies the La Salle purred between
the rows of Russian olive trees on the way to a second dessert:
lemon sherbet at the dairy or apple pie at Dillworth's cousin's
house. Until the cousin had a child, and they stopped going.
"Babies are far too new and sudden," Dillworth said.

For a few years he stalled off the future and even allowed
himself to be carefree about it. In the summer of 1938, when

Nettie was fifty-three and they had been married eight years, he asked if she would like to take a trip East, and she said: "It doesn't matter. If you'd like, dear." She had learned to take direction well, and convinced herself the trip was a good idea even if her digestion was bad in strange water and she knew she would not sleep on thick, new mattresses. Dillworth, who always picked out her clothes, found at Haskel and Porteus a most acceptable navy-blue polka-dot jersey and a lavender redingote

.   .   .

The trip Eas
was long. Ohio windfalls stirred by the Battleship Gray car were whirls of fallen apples and yellow leaves. The sky was full of gifts, and all the disappeared August days burst fulfilled upon September, confusing goldenrod and bumblebees that had given up on summer. Nettie and Dillworth had run out of compliments for the season's personal generosity, long past "nice, isn't it?" "lovely and warm," "just what the doctor ordered," even the jolly "when the frost is on the pumpkin, mother." They leaned back on the cushions and let themselves be taken.

They stopped in New York for two days to walk baffled through penny arcades on Broadway and past the dinosaur bones in the natural history museum. On the Chinatown tour Nettie got sick from the lamb chop and baked potato —she wouldn't eat any of the gray messes in covered dishes. They got their money back on that, and were not disappointed in Radio City and the Rainbow Room.

Back on Route 1 they constantly stopped for chocolate

malteds in Rexalls that smelled of disinfectant. They priced bathing caps and sun-tan lotion because they were approaching the sea, and in the height of exuberance rented a beach house for two weeks at a resort with a long Indian name.

•   •   •

The cottage at first seemed terribly empty. "It's only for the rest of the month," Dillworth repeated, in the voice people reserve for things they can not believe in. They had never before lived in a place that belonged to somebody else, and it was both exciting and ominous, as if they might suddenly be losing their pasts and going on as nomads to one-night stands. The houses they grew up in had furniture selected generations before; even the pictures had been hung before they were born; shoes and mandolins and cribbage boards belonging to long-dead relatives were in attic trunks. They had never thought of buying anything new; it would have seemed disloyal.

The front porch of the gray cottage had buckets of summer-worn geraniums and a glider upon which, one afternoon in their second week there, Nettie sat. From the back of the cottage, in the kitchen, Dillworth could see the flat salt pond meandering among the marsh grass. At low tide, when the distracting sound of the surf had died, it was, he thought, just like home, just like Cottonwood Pond. From the front Nettie's little voice worried about his turning the two chops, hers rare, his well-done. She was wearing her powder-blue rajah silk with the ruching tied down by a bowknot pin made of a sapphire crowned with seed pearls. Her feet could not touch the sandy porch planks. She was almost through Anne Morrow Lindbergh's *North to the Orient*: the Yangtze had overflowed and the two brave, handsome Americans were mapping the disaster area and dropping medical supplies. It was beautifully sad.

For two days wet clouds had hung despondent over the dead sand; the marsh grass was flat and the children's voices next door had gone limp. A couple of fishermen squeaked along the fringe of the sudsy sea.

"It *is* messy, isn't it?" she asked when Dillworth came out again.

The ocean was being unusually generous, but in secondhand objects: swollen oranges, tar-striped sneakers, angry tangles of weed, more undefinable objects that had been churned together so long they had lost their identity and now, flushed here, were dank and gelid. The gulls fell behind in cleaning up and were easily distracted.

"My chop, Dilly," she warned.

"It's hard to keep your mind on any one thing for ten minutes," he said, banging the screen door.

•   •   •

The waves
broke hugely on the beach and then scuttled back as if they were going to be beaten for daring so much. Hundreds rolled together into one coarse green mass. The frothy edge covered all the oranges, corks, sneakers, fish-and-man garbage. It rose beyond the seaweed line. The highest spongy ladders

licked at the points of dune grass. The day grew darker, and
indecision rolled audibly in Nettie's big stomach. She looked
in through the porch window to see whether Dillworth had
set the table yet.

He hadn't. He was watching the couple next door piling
their summer goods into a throbbing Plymouth. He did not
think about it then, but it was odd they were making such a
frenzied departure from a rented beach house on a Wednesday afternoon when their lease ran through Saturday. What
had offended him was their reckless loading of that car—a
layer of paper bags and sheets freshly torn from beds, then a
layer of children. Even birds, he thought, leave more dis-
creetly, gather quietly on telephone wires, practice-dive a
couple of times, and then, cautioned and encouraged by wise
leaders, swish off without one disheveled feather. That some
ingredient of success was inbred in birds but missing in people did not surprise Dillworth. When the last paper bag had
been thrown into the Plymouth and the dog had been told to
crawl in where he could find room, the people drove away,
up the narrow dirt road toward the nearest town. They
neither waved nor looked in his direction. They had asked him
their first night to come over for bridge or poker or whatever
he'd like, and he had told them what he'd really like was to
have them keep their Boston terrier out of his garbage pail.
After that they were decidedly cool. He had had experiences
with pushy neighbors in Grand Island. He could never know
how they'd turn out, and until he could see them finally
turned out, he wanted nothing to do with them.

Nettie was at his shoulder. She seldom came into the

kitchen. "The waves are very high—almost on the front steps. What can we do about the car?" They had taken the cottage because it had a basement garage.

"They will go down. There is a high tide and a low tide every day." He had told her that before, but she was unconvinced.

"I think I like the plains better. You can be sure of them." Although agreeing, he did not add anything. "If you look out this window, it's like home." He had noticed that. On good days a low wind parted the hairy marsh grass, and it reminded him of fields of oats or wheat. Now, thick, angry gusts, curtains of sharp spray, crisscrossed the field, shrouding the bluffs beyond.

"We will eat here, in the kitchen," he said, and served their chops with beach-plum jelly. While they were eating the last spoonfuls of lemon sponge, a flat thudding began on the front porch, as if someone were opening and closing the screen door faster and faster. A great paw seemed to be slapping the house, and in the front, glass splintered delicately.

When he ran to the living room, he saw water licking at the feet of the wicker furniture. It was ridiculous until he remembered the Battleship Gray La Salle underneath.

Nettie said, "We'll have to go up to the bedroom," and they climbed the stairs after Dillworth had put the dishes in the sink and turned on the faucet (but no water ran).

They had spent little time in the bedroom. It was like the attic in Grand Island, bare pine rafters and unfinished walls cushioned with heat in midday. Now it was cold and very dark and straining in the undecided wind. Dillworth thought he saw deepening waves where the road to town should have been, but a thick glaze of rain and spray coated the window.

"I suppose," Nettie said, "the car will be ruined." Before this she had always called it the La Salle. "We could pray, Dillworth."

"Yes, we could." But they did not. There was little to do but lie on the mattress, shut their eyes, and vainly think themselves at home. After one circular thrust, the house gave up and tilted. The bed slid toward the window as if they were in a carnival funhouse, and water began to pour from the floor and sides.

When it was as high as the bed springs, it lifted the mattress gently and Dillworth said: "When you can reach them, hold tight to the rafters." Which she did, a white arm frantic around the pine beam.

There was still enough light from the broken window and the holes in the sides of the attic to let him see her face, and he was astonished by its incredible youthfulness. He could never have looked as young as she did at the moment when, without making a sound, she gave up and seemed to lie back on the bed of black water. That was what he thought about as he crouched in the triangle of the rafters until the tides receded and the rescue workers' flashlight beams struck his face.

National attention fell on the survivors, and through no particular action they became famous, like miners pulled from crumbled shafts. A great morgue was set up in the high school gymnasium, and a Red Cross worker cautiously loaded Dillworth onto a westbound train.

•   •   •

The old age
of Dillworth Plante had already begun. His doctor was fond
of telling the nurse after his frequent examinations: "That
man has the oldest body you'll ever see. I don't know how he
manages." Dillworth was always getting lost in the supermarket and not looking to the left when he crossed streets.
Those unlucky children who were cast as grandfathers in
school pageants followed him, learning how to be old. When
he died at fifty, several years ago, they did not put the age
in the obituary because no one would have believed it.

JUST TELL ME

ALL YOUR

TROUBLES

❧❦❧ The spring George Dietz met the Morses they were expanding their circle. His first meetings with them remained clearly defined and separate as color slides. He had gone to a Sunday morning Bartók concert in an interdenominational church and had been claimed at the coffee hour afterward. Like most of the morning's congregation he had come for the Bartók; generally, they were the unbelieving middle-aged children of churchgoing parents, and they sat uneasily, guilty of being in any church on a Sunday morning and confused by this strange redwood barn in the center of which intense musicians like grasshoppers stretched their nervous arms, spotlights reflected in their glasses. Jagged edges of the music bounced off and around the rigid listeners, who, resurrected after the program, poured loudly into a large reception hall.

George was so grateful for the coffee that he moved to the windows and smiled at a tall girl in a sacky dress who was leaning against the draperies.

"I haven't seen you at morning reflections before. Are you new?" When she spoke, George had to bend toward her low voice. All the women he knew were either shrill or crisp.

"Oh, I've been around for a year or so," he answered, "but busy, not really living. This is like coming up for air. So I suppose I am new to anybody but me."

"How come? You don't look especially water-logged." He studied her lips as if he were deaf. She was wearing no makeup; her face was large and soft, her full lips were spread wide over fine small teeth. The large glasses and her severe hair made her look like a good child trying to impress influential relatives.

"Well, I've been working on a project." It was impossible to describe the only focus his mind and muscles had owned for a year. It was impossible to explain that a grown man had worried most of the waking hours of ten months over a pile of blueprints, oblivious to the whole city or the country. Meanwhile, all over the city, life had been led; old men in greasy hats had eaten blue-plate specials and had had strokes climbing onto the front stoops, and were now buried under thin new grass; babies had been conceived, born, named, and paraded in front of smiling aunts; men and women who would have passed each other as strangers the autumn before were that Sunday morning snoring against each other.

"My thesis project took a lot longer than it should have."

"What is it all about?" she asked, but looked at the same time into the damp garden where the forsythia bunched.

"City planning. It started as a complex of middle-priced apartments, but then my advisor thought I should fill in the school and the stores and all the landscaping."

"Like creating a little world."

"That's right. But now that I've come out I wonder why I ever thought I had anything to say. What's been standing here and lived in up and down these streets looks good enough for another century."

"Spring has that effect. It shakes you up and makes you feel all the winter concerns were sort of useless."

"I had forgottten about the possibilities of spring. I wondered why the light was getting better every day. You don't hear the hylas in the city."

"There are a lot of them here in the park along with the wild geese. It's not the same as seeing the geese in a sunset sky out in the country, discussing whether to try another twenty miles or to bed down in this strange pond for the night. You have to look harder for signs of spring here, but that makes it worth the looking."

"You've lived here a long time?" he asked.

"No, only the most important part. My name's Emily Morse, and I live near the park. Why don't you walk me home?"

George, who was bold only in retrospect and in dreams, chewed his lips before he nodded.

They walked along the Sunday streets to her house in an area that could have been a case book in reclamation: a shoe repair with a sleeping cat and a dusty assortment of heels, wax, soles, and laces; a couple of three-decker apartment houses; an empty store on whose soaped windows smiled the defeated candidates of a fall election; a sagging colonial shingled in beige tar paper; and here and there bright restorations waiting to swallow up the street. One of these was Emily's gray Victorian chalet with long peaked windows.

As the red door was opened, she announced: "This is my husband, Henry."

Henry waved them into the living room. "I'm doing the *Times* crossword. My Sunday worship service—the *Times* and E. Power Biggs."

"You talk with George and I'll heat up some stew." She glided into a darker part of the house and began rattling dishes.

George sat on the edge of a green velvet chair. "It's a big imposition, my barging in like this."

"We never eat alone. Emily always has someone in tow. It's like open house year round. That's what a house is for, isn't it—to fill it with people? We never even lock the door."

Henry was a stout man who made wide gestures and whose voice washed the room in good will.

"I should think," George said, "you'd have problems not looking up."

"What do you mean?"

"Being robbed." Seeing Henry wince at the world, he hurried on. "I mean, people are careless, picking up things that don't belong."

"Locks are a sign of contempt for human beings. Locked doors are illicit temptations. What we have to do is reason and share. About a year ago Emily found a kid, not ten years old, at that hall table, bending over her pocketbook. He needed the money—where can a ten-year-old get fifteen dollars honestly? So Emily gave it to him on condition that he

would stay for lunch and go downtown with her and spend
the money. Look." Henry picked up a latticed wooden tray.
"He made this for us when we sent him to day camp last
summer. Three hundred popsicle sticks glued together."

Henry fondled the tray, his eyes swimming, and George
wondered how to praise this earnest good man enough. Since
he could think of nothing appropriate, he smiled out at the
white room, where fiberglass curtains trembled at the long
windows and ferns grew abundantly in great ceramic jardi-
nieres. In a large cage some brightly colored birds shifted and
stretched their wings but did not sing.

Emily's stew was somewhat thin, but along with it came
great chunks of bread. "Makes it fresh every Friday," Henry
said, bending toward her between mouthfuls and kissing her.

George continued to smile while he ate; the life he had
neglected for a year crowded close, within grasping distance.
The things he had missed and the people he had abandoned:
his own parents, the crying child in the apartment below, the
men in his college fraternity, his best friend in grade school.
The difficulty was knowing where to begin, and he had to
study the methods and the language as if he had been paralyzed. While the afternoon eroded, the Morses' hi-fi delivered
Mozart quartets very loudly and there was no need to talk.

At one point George looked toward the hall and thought
he saw an angry face pressed against the door. "Is that someone for you?" he asked. The Morses roused themselves from
the sofa, where they were dozing like cats.

"I'll go. It's probably José," Henry said. After a long discussion with the invisible visitor he shouted through the

screen door: "I'm going to walk José back to his place. I'll be back in a little while."

Emily gazed after him thoughtfully.

"I must go," George said. "Good Lord, I've been here four hours. You should have told me. What you must be thinking about me."

Emily's great eyes widened under the thick glasses, and she rubbed her arms nervously. "Oh please, don't leave me. It will take Henry all night. José wouldn't come in here because he could smell a stranger, and he's completely possessive about us. Poor fellow has the most awful problems."

George tried not to look interested and became absorbed in squaring a pile of magazines.

"At this moment," she went on, "the only way to help José is to listen while he talks himself out. So many pieces of his life have been falling into place, and he's suddenly discovered that there's more to existence than parking cars all day. He used to work in a parking lot next to the building where Henry's office is and one day Henry asked him if he was happy and if he was going to spend the rest of his life fitting a hundred cars into ninety spaces. So I guess he started thinking about the future and he decided to become a real person and asked Henry where to start. Oh—what do you care about all this?"

"Go on. It's fascinating." He was shamelessly sincere. "If only you knew how much I care about everything alive, everything."

"Not any more than we do. People are for us the greatest reason for being."

"What did Henry advise José to do?"

Delighted by his interest, she sat on the camel saddle in front of his chair, her arms around her knees. "Henry is a great believer in self-fulfillment, you know, uniting the vocation to the avocation. So he encouraged José to take a life drawing course at the Adult Education Center, and he was good, terribly good, twenty years ahead of the ladies with blue hair that sketch on Tuesday nights. And he really wanted to know himself, to read and think, you know. For twelve years he was driving hundreds of thousands of miles on one acre of asphalt, and most of it in reverse. What a rotten deal! So—he got himself fired in order to qualify for unemployment and so he could walk along the river at eleven o'clock in the morning if he felt like it."

George was sobered by the tragedy of millions of the dutiful employed who almost never had the chance to see the river at eleven o'clock in the morning and who finally died without knowing anything at all.

"That's what I should do," he thought and said aloud at the same time, "get a time extension for the thesis. Finish it in the summer and take stock now."

"Yes, you should try getting out of yourself more. How can you be a meaningful city planner, if you don't see the human beings you're planning for? We'll introduce you to all our friends."

That is how George became part of the circle and began seeing so much of the Morses that it was hard to remember that he had not always known them. They filled picnic baskets with food he had mentioned liking and drove him to look at interesting new shopping centers. He bought them expensive wine, took them to the symphony, found a porcelain stove from Salzburg in an antique shop and spent a week painting it as a birthday gift for Emily. When he was not telephoning or eating or walking with the Morses, he thought a great deal about them. He had taken several rolls of color film of them on their excursions and, when alone, often shuffled through them. It was strange to spy on the Morses this way; they were such restless, mobile people, but when George wanted to think of them, he could consider them as they were in the photographs.

Together, they talked endlessly about their childhoods, about college, about the *real* point of life, and when George came back to his room long after midnight his tongue was sore. But in his head the dialogue continued, and lured by the need to share everything in his head the next morning he would walk with embarrassing speed toward the park and their house.

Once there, he would listen; Henry was a great talker and a believer in the healing power of speech. Coming up the front steps, you could hear the fine seamless sliding and rustling of his voice. There were no silences, and often when George thought he had found a gap in the forest of sentences and tried to walk through, the effort died in his throat as Henry began again.

It was Emily who listened as if her whole body could absorb the sound and meaning. "Tell me," she asked, "about your father training the beagles in West Virginia." "Why," her voice hesitated on the telephone, "don't you come with me this morning? We could shop and do the laundry and then you could try a lentil soup I just finished before you get back to the desk." If George failed to join her, Henry would appear suddenly on his way home from the office. "I happened to buy this bourbon for next to nothing. Ever see this brand before? Let's take it over to my place and try it."

Usually José ate dinner with them, and then Henry talked less while José described waiting in line for the unemployment checks on Friday and how only one window at the agency was open and how a slow fat official interviewed him in a voice loud enough for anyone to hear. They dramatized the whole scene, Emily and Henry played the line of unemployed, George was cast as José, and José was the fat official thumping and wheezing through a lecture to the lazy drones of the world.

It is easy to lose one spring, and even simpler to use up a summer without a trace. George thought of his thesis project constantly but did less about it every day. Habits spread themselves like lichens over his day—waiting for the morning paper, waiting for the mail, cooking lunch, hoping that the Morses wouldn't call, then wondering why they hadn't, and, finally, calling them to find out what they were doing. When it was safely five o'clock and nothing more than the nothing he had produced could be expected of the day, he became momentarily happy with it.

In August even the filmy curtains refused to quiver but reflected the burning pavement outside. The ageratum and geraniums turned brown; the petunias dangled into vines. The Morses and two of their circle were going to the shore

for a couple of weeks; one Saturday night George helped them
load a borrowed station wagon with books and clothes and
promised to water their philodendron, collect the mail, and
feed the birds. Henry leaned against the car and stared up at
the street light circled with thick green leaves and shabby
moths. "I wish you'd come with us. You could do a lot of
work. We'd leave you alone all day."

"Yes," Emily said. "We could all have schedules, study
hours in the morning, swimming and bird-watching in the
afternoon."

"No," George tried to say firmly, "I had all that when I was
a kid at camp, and I was almost as lazy then as I am now."

When he awakened that Sunday morning, birds were
singing outside. He thought they were scolding a cat, but
they were simply singing over some private joy, and that
seemed a good omen. He ate a large breakfast and contem-
plated the day and the two weeks beyond with gratitude.
He believed luck ran in waves and was determined to ride
this great swell as far as it would go. He would do nothing to
disturb the pattern, not wash a cup or read a word of the
newspaper or think about the water shortage or the significance of his life. The luck ran incredibly well; by noon he had
designed several acres of off-street parking and as the light
dimmed and night came he had landscaped the pedestrian
mall.

In the middle of the next afternoon he remembered the
Morses' mail and their birds and plants. Inside their house,
a dusty silence covered the Swedish divan and the Finnish
hangings. The place smelled deserted. Had he ever sat on the

shaggy rug and leaned against the drum coffee table and shouted about the UN or socialized medicine or unilateral disarmament? The kitchen sink was dry and the garbage can empty. He stood at the door of the Morses' bedroom: the bed was covered with a batik throw, the edges sloped down tiredly, the middle was depressed into a hammock. Emily's cleaning was always slapdash and left fingerprints on the bureau, grease spots on the carpet, wide-spread bobby pins on the bathroom floor, curls of dust under the radiator. It might have been anyone's locked-up house; without the Morses even the Picasso prints and the Swedish furniture emphasized its commonness. George wondered how anyone left his mark on objects and was frightening himself by recognizing his own insignificance when the hall telephone began ringing. He thought of leaving the house suddenly and not answering it. They had not told him what to do about the telephone. After staring at it for a while, he answered.

Coins crashed and fell on the other end, and Emily's summer-happy voice called out: "Found you. We've been calling every hour since morning."

Henry had taken the phone. "How're you doing? Look, we think you ought to come down to Sioscutt."

Emily's voice in the background: "Tell him we need his stabilizing influence. Tell him we have barrels of room. Tell him how quiet it is and how we're having wonderful weather."

"How about coming down?" Henry asked.

"Oh, I'm getting along very well. I'm working hard, honestly." It was too frivolous and personal to use a long-distance call to talk about malls and parking lots. So he leaned against the wall listening to Henry's and Emily's pleas and leafing through their Florentine leather-bound book of telephone numbers. By now he could identify most of them. Lois Sakoski, a big dazed girl who worked in Henry's office and who lived with an alcoholic mother. The mother occasionally broke out of the locked house, and once George had been sent to bring her home from a supermarket where she had thrown dozens of soup cans at the other customers.

"You'll work ever so much more efficiently down here," Henry promised. "The other night I wrote out a menu of the meals we could have next week. Now pay attention, boy, while the chef appeals to your basest needs."

Emily had grabbed the telephone. "He doesn't care about food. Let me talk with him. George, you've just got to come. We need you."

George had to blot out the long pause after this. He had always been a good boy, following instructions well. In recent years he was seldom asked to do anything directly. It was easy to please the Morses. Therefore he responded cheerfully and quickly: "All right, I'll come."

Henry and Emily competed to show their enthusiasm by shouting about what they would eat and what movies they would see together. While he reminded them that it would be an expensive call, George became more pleased with the rightness of his decision. Other people went on vacations with their friends to the sea and the mountains; his friends had summoned him and he would join them the next day. The simplicity and rightness of this overwhelmed him. He gathered up the cage, in which the surprised birds swung gravely on their trapeze.

The next morning in the weedy parking lot behind the apartment building he tried starting his car. For the last year when he remembered it and was willing to spend several minutes starting it by an elaborate ritual of hand and foot action, it would percolate rustily a few blocks and then shudder back into the old parking space. This time the engine refused to awaken.

While he had been driving around in the coughing car, he had assumed that the train stations were buzzing with people, that porters struggled with mounded suitcases, and that the big cavern echoed with muffled announcements of arrivals and departures. But he found that the silent interior was crossed by dusty rays of gritty sunlight. The restaurant was boarded up; the sign announcing departures was smudged. Sailors and old men in drooping felt hats shuffled through abandoned newspapers in the waiting pews. They were momentarily curious about anyone taking such a large bird cage onto a train.

In George's imagination the idea of a trip was necessarily frivolous. He awaited congratulations on his daring or accusations on his lack of principle in abandoning work. He searched for some way to express his festive mood, but the weighing machine was stuck at 299 and a lounging policeman in the men's room stared warily at him. Still, even aboard the grubby train he kept his enthusiasm, despite bullet holes in the windows and gashes in the seats. Nothing would put him out of the holiday style, not any pink-cheeked old conductor marked for death. He bought a slab of mummified cake from the round-shouldered dwarf lugging sixteen tons of sandwiches and coffee through the coach. "Look alive. You're going on a holiday," he whispered to the birds. "Wait, I'll get it," he shouted at a baffled strong woman shoving a little case onto the rack. George, the Great-hearted, George the Good Sport, smiled at crying babies and pimpled youths while he played the merry man on excursion. Slumping carefully, he watched the hazy flatlands run to the sea and studied patronizingly the anchored boats.

So few trains ran to Sioscutt that each arrival resembled a carnival. Emily and Henry in very unpressed madras took his arms and nodded to a sullen girl. "José's in the car, and this is Maud Flanagan."

During the drive toward the beach they advanced schemes for George's working. Emily, who never woke up before nine o'clock, was sure that you worked best in the cool hours before sunrise. José was for sleeping through the days and having the good quiet hours of the night to yourself. Maud was silent, her white-gray eyes busy with the floor of the car or some distant horizon the others couldn't see. They pointed out summer landmarks, the laundermat, where they got beer or bought the Sunday *Times*.

"Be especially nice to Maud," Emily whispered to George. "She's had absolutely rotten luck; really unbelievable."

"She does look out of it."

"Being here has done wonders for her. Now that you've come, the family's complete. Everything will be wonderful."

George waded through the happiness. He had such a supply of it, it was selfish not to give away quantities. One had only to find out what brand the other people needed.

There was hardly room for Henry to drive along the main

street of Sioscutt with the skinny kids in sandy bathing suits delicately placing their feet against the hot tar and their mothers bulging out of orange slacks. Tents and trailers touched each other in the fields opposite the sea. When the rusty hinges squeaked open on their cabin, the inside was an ocean of beds covered with flowered spreads and holding the thick smell of old sneakers.

"Tonight we'll let you work," Emily promised, but of course it was his first night and he couldn't really desert them. Also, despite his concern and worry, two of the birds had died on the trip and he was searching for ways to be nicer to the Morses.

So they went to O'Leary's to join the crowd of lifeguards, surfers, and bass fishermen, milling around a small TV screen where celebrities in evening dress played charades for penny prizes. The audio was either broken or lost in the hedge of talk around the bar. George, with delicate politeness, leaned against the wall beside Maud. She held a transistor radio over one ear under a cascade of streaked hair and stared at the table top.

"Make-believe music?" he asked. "Could we hear a little?"

"Some people want everything." She turned further away from him. "Why bother?"

"I've never had one."

"One what?"

"A transistor radio. I've never owned one."

"Then why don't you go buy one?"

That seemed to end the conversation. Emily rewarded him by a thin smile and later with a conspiratory conversation on the boardwalk outside O'Leary's.

"You've been fabulously patient with Maud. I wasn't going to tell you what happened, but it explains the way she is."

"I don't really want to know." Her lowered eyes showed that he had shut off some admittedly fascinating revelation. "I mean, it's none of my business what's chewing her up inside. Anyway, she's your friend and Henry's and I haven't any right to analyze her."

"You're one of our family now," Emily said and caught his arm fast in hers. They walked along the stony edges of the beach where the feeble low tide lapped. "That's why you had to come, so we'd be together. All weekend only half of me was here. The other part was there watching you and worrying about whether you'd be lonely or eat enough. Henry said he felt the same way. When you're pulled apart, how do you know which you is the real one."

"You and Henry shouldn't worry so much about other people. We'd take care of ourselves, not as well as you do, but we'd stay alive."

"Well, you're here. That's all that matters now. These stones are killing my feet. Let's go sit up there."

From inside O'Leary's the jukebox was spilling out Petula Clark. An electric guitar whined everybody's happy pain. It was surprisingly light on the dunes. George, who was a little uneasy at being alone here with Emily, began picking wild roses and lupine and entwining them into a small braid.

"Let me dress up in these," she said and tied the flower chains around her neck and wrists. "How is your thesis project coming?"

He was glad that she had asked, but when he finished describing the pedestrian mall, he wondered if that was all he

had been spending his days on. Telling about it diminished
its size and value. Emily was trying, he knew, to look interested; she had arched her head at him and stopped playing
with the flower garlands.

"What happened to your advisor? His name was Steinberger, wasn't it?"

"I haven't seen him for a while, not after I got the extension. I was ashamed, but now that I've made some progress,
I'll drop by the office."

"Did Dr. Steinberger have a daughter?" she asked absently.

"I don't know. I just wouldn't have thought of asking.
Our advisors are awfully remote."

"It seems to me that I heard something about his child
being very sick. But it could have been some other Steinberger."

"He's the kind of man you could easily forget. Deferential
and sort of bland on the surface, suits so well tailored and
tended that they're never old or new, his hair never freshly
cut or needing a trim. In the first place he probably wouldn't
have children, and if he did, they'd be high-grade plastic."

When they got back to O'Leary's, José was dancing bril-
liantly with a teenager in a purple shift. Henry was leaning
across the table trying to tell Maud about the surface of the
moon.

"Some people say it's fuzzy; some think it's rocky or
covered with all the dust that we would sweep up here. Perhaps it's like a marshmallow or a feather bed. You know, the
other day I was reading the most interesting item about the
amount of infection we would be responsible for when we
go to the other planets. We can give them all our diseases,

and of course they can give us new kinds that we haven't had. Isn't that fascinating?"

Maud did not apparently think so, but turned to Emily in her garlands.

"Well, look at the Queen of the May."

Emily took them off. "They'd look better on you."

"They're all wilted," Maud said. "Nothing's meant to last beside the sea, not sand castles or flowers or people."

That was her most extensive statement during George's week at the cottage. At night she and Emily slept in one room on creaky iron beds, and George and Henry lay in the other room waiting for the light and for José's return.

"Poor José is finally getting a divorce," Emily explained one morning.

"And it's about time," Henry added.

"I didn't even know he was married," George said.

"Oh, yes, she was a cheap little tramp, greedy and egocentric as they come. All she cared about was the unemployment check and when it gave out she left too. But that was just typical of the pattern of José's life. A sensitive man with all that potential tied to a piece of scum."

Every night José danced grimly and endlessly with the girl in purple.

George had opened his eyes on the first morning to a soupy mass of fog that seemed to have invaded the cottage. The edges of the following days were draped in fog; in the center of the days drizzle fell, and the men gathered wood for the outdoor fireplace. Their stretch of the beach was entirely domesticated; in many ways it resembled a hall closet: pieces of plastic, colored sponges, milk cartons, orange skins, and slabs of wood were everywhere. The wood was not old, but entirely new, freshly torn from houses and boats before weathering.

The beach became a winter resort. Wrapped up like Arabs, they sat around the bonfires between the squalls. The doors of cottages slammed and opened, revealing the anguish of pent-up children and dogs, and the damp chairs and beds released the smells of all past summers. The most sensible people were the bass fishermen, shrouded in canvas, who squished home at midnight to warm beds.

Maud tried to live on the edges of their routine. When she went for a walk, Emily turned an anxious face and took off over the dunes, after which Maud would stalk back alone. One day George saw Maud scudding fiercely back through the sand followed by a breathless Emily.

"I was only trying to help. I thought you wanted company," Emily explained.

"But I need to be alone. All of us spend the day stretched out on our cots, sighing and scratching our heads like monkeys in some third-rate zoo. It's getting on my nerves."

"We understand, Maud. Of course, it's hard starting again."

With all her sadness gathered tight inside her body, Maud made herself into a statue. "So he killed himself. You didn't even know him." She cradled one hand in the other. "This has been a wake, and not one of you knew the corpse. But everyone's squeaking around, trying to keen for a man you never laid eyes on."

"You're just over-nervous about it. That makes you defensive."

"I'm not defensive and not guilty, and at the rate you've been grieving, he's been mourned enough, and by strangers."

"We never wanted to make you feel guilty. We're proud of your being brave, but it was a traumatic experience."

"How long can you keep a trauma alive? Even when you pick a scab off every day, you get a welt at the end."

George heard them outside the window; he pretended great absorption in the vat of sweet corn he was steaming. No one was especially interested in food, and fish were surprisingly more expensive on the wharf than they were in city super-markets, but he believed that it was decent and proper to eat the food of the region. He brought back to the cottage five lobsters that rattled inside their bag and jars of salt water in which to boil them. It gave him a few hours respite from worrying about more important matters. But at dinner the others did not finish the lobsters and poked apprehen-sively at the liver and roe and decided the shell was too much work to break. What was left decayed vividly through the week in the garbage, but no one referred to the smell.

George tried working in various places which had seemed effective before being tried, open windows with a view of the fog or without, benches under a pine tree, dunes, the beach itself. But with the rain and wind and mists and cold his designing of apartments and offices became more irrelevant daily. "We should have stayed in caves. Or maybe remained nomadic. We were better off on camels," he said aloud into the dark room full of beds.

When they came back from Sioscutt, there were only a few more days of summer. As he was telling Emily how his mother had always put away the white dresses and shoes and taken the slip covers off on Labor Day, he realized that it was September. "My God, it's all over, and I've only done the mall and the parking. How am I going to face Steinberger?"

"You still have a couple of weeks before school opens. Anyway, why not ask for an extension? Everybody does."

"I've already had one. The longer I put it off, the later I'll get a job. The money I saved won't last much longer."

Emily said very carefully what she must have thought about before this. "We don't have a lot, but anything we have, you know is yours to share. You can pay anytime."

He tried to protest. In the past he had been the kind of man who always kept his watch fifteen minutes fast and turned the calendar pages before the next month had really begun. Often he had made out checks in advance and put them in envelopes with penciled notes clipped on: Send next Thursday. Hold until July 1.

The week before registration he went to see Steinberger. The university had slept through its first century, but now had busily taken over several schools that it housed in asphalt blocks bordered by thin trees, freshly planted and reluctant to grow. The concrete buildings were unusually dark inside. Their few windows were slits; tunnels connected the buildings so that the entire mass resembled a fort under seige.

Steinberger's secretary, like most of the departmental secretaries, was a graduate student's wife, awaiting the completion of a thesis before respectability could begin in terms of babies and a station wagon to be piloted to Little League, trumpet lessons, and stamp redemption centers. That work was intolerable agony and endurable only for those blessed ends showed in every gesture and in her terrible reluctance to begin typing a long letter or sorting the mail, lest there not be time to finish. She also remained surprised that anyone would take education seriously.

"Oh, you wanted to see Dr. Steinberger? He should be in his office. Why don't you just ask if he's free?"

In George's stomach rocks slid against each other. His feet seemed impossibly far from his nerves, but somehow, with the crisp wife staring, he made it down the hall to knock at Steinberger's door.

"You'll have to make more noise than that," she said, and when he had thrown his fist against the door again, something answered and he walked in.

"I'd be grateful if you'd see me for a few minutes."

"You're here, aren't you? What is it you want?"

George knew that Steinberger couldn't place him. "My name's Dietz. I'm in the planning curriculum, and I've been working on a suburban renewal project."

"Well, did you bring it with you?"

"No. That is—I almost did, but finally I didn't."

Steinberger's eyes were fixed outside his slit of a window. The office was a neat place: only a glassed-in bookcase and five travel posters from clean and successful German and Danish cities. George could find nothing here or in his churning head to drag out for discussion.

"What did you do with it?" Steinberger asked.

"With what, sir?"

"The spring and the summer and most of the fall. What

did you do with them? You're going to let the government support you the rest of your life. I know your type, know them too well. Going from grant to grant, never doing one damn thing the rest of your life and criticizing everybody that ever breathed. I used to think we needed people like you, but I'm not so sure now. It may be that we just need the big stupid well-disciplined guys that sit in the front row and snap their fingers at you and yell 'Doc, hey, doc, I know' when you ask rhetorical questions. What's wrong with you, anyway?"

"Nothing, really. The time just got away from me."

"I suppose it was socializing. You're not married, are you?"

"No." George was trying to remember if statistics indicated that the best city planners were married at the beginning or at the end of graduate work. It was no use. His mind had grown too fat and loose to think, and fear slowly seeped through all his bones.

"Well, I'm sorry to have bothered you." As he backed out of the office, he was alarmed to notice, or thought he did, that Steinberger's eyes were wet.

"Edgy," the secretary said. "He's going to pieces. It's his child, you know."

"I didn't know he had one."

"Just the one. She's dying of leukemia, and he's trying to blight as much of the world as he can."

"How awful."

"They say you can get used to anything if you wait long enough."

George stared at Steinberger's door. "Is there anything to do? Should I tell him I could do something?"

"What did you have in mind—making like God or something? Look," she said, leaning over her typewriter, "you have problems you haven't used. Why don't you go and worry about them?"

"All right," he said. "I'll go worry right now." But in order to worry properly, focus is necessary, and his mind was too scattered. It kept running around smelling out fresh horrors.

In the dark corridors, trophy cases, lockers, telephone booths, photographs of campus queens, and coffee machines sped by. How can we, he thought, be so long in school and every year be more frightened by it? This is one more of man's tortures. As if nature is not fierce enough with storms and age and disease, we design snares and hand out traffic tickets, life sentences, and failures—always failures.

Once he was outside the university blockhouse, there seemed to be more air. Peaceful pictures lighted in his head for a second and then vanished: his nice chunky parents who were impossible to disappoint, eating hearty meals and then playing double solitaire on the Quaker lace draped dining room table; his good brothers-in-law on Sundays at the zoo lifting their heavy children high to see the polar bear cubs; his worried high school teachers talking about their college days; all the good, disappointed sufferers securely married to their burdens and their little pleasures. He was the only loathsome stranger wandering outside the walls. Something has happened to me, George thought, my toenails are turning yellow and my mouth tastes sour. Ever since spring I have been sinking, but I will pull myself together.

He did try every morning—for a diminishing number of

distracted minutes. He watched the hours pass by. Processions on the street outside marked the sweep of time: first, men in heavy suits with attaché cases, then clumps of purposeful children bent toward the model school at the university, then their shopping mothers pulling wire laundry carts, dogs and old people scratching unevenly along, and then all the tribes in reversed order. Each group nudged his guilt again, and he would fill with enthusiasm that drained before the accusers had faded out of hearing.

Most of all, he began to dread the Morses—whether he saw them or didn't. Maud and José had been eating up their days. José's wife was contesting the divorce; since she would have attached his pay, he did not work, but lived at the Moses. Emily had found a cut-rate analyst who agreed to see Maud at seven-thirty in the morning before his regular practice. Then it was necessary to persuade Maud to appreciate the bargain, and that used up several days. When Maud discovered resemblances between him and her lover of the winter before, the analyst turned directive. The directiveness concentrated on methods of purging Maud's selfishness: she became a volunteer in a state home for the feeble-minded. Her reluctance was monumental. Henry and George had to drive her through the pretty campus of the institution to her assignment. In front of the red brick cottage they spent several minutes each morning exhorting her out of the car onto the swings where her stolid charges waited in their unpressed cotton dresses, some of them clutching seedy-looking dolls.

"See, they're all waiting for you, Maud," Henry would say cheerfully. "They're all looking forward to your playing with them."

Then George would coax her out of the car. "Come on,
Maud. It's not so bad."

He tentatively shoved one of the dumpy and expressionless women into the air. What was the use? What was he good
for anyway?

When he asked Emily, she explained. "You're good for us,
for Henry, Maud, and me." His goodness was subtle enough
not to be visible. When he took Maud to the movies, she left
a seat between them; when the Morses sent them for a walk,
she dragged along absorbed in the trees or the street lights.

One morning when Emily was leading a group of Japanese
nursing students from the university on a tour of historical
houses, Maud drew two hundred dollars from the Morses'
checking account and left for Los Angeles by Greyhound.
Emily cried as she passed trays of hickory smoked cheese
and crackers at the Japanese girls, who lifted their expressionless faces like saucers at her.

"Stay for lunch. Oh, please stay for lunch," she asked, but
all the narrow eyes widened in clear protest. They fled like
elegant, expensive birds she had been lucky to borrow for a
morning.

At first George did not answer the telephone. But he had
nowhere to go to escape. To economize and hoping to find
inspiration, he had moved to another part of the city, as far
away from the Morses and the university as it was possible to
get. He was living in one room over a dry cleaner's.

Emily's low sad voice filled the telephone. "Maud didn't
even leave a note. I don't know what bothered her. I always asked her to share her problems, to talk them out.
You know, it's not the money, but the fact that she would

not tell us what the matter was. What do you think it was?"

"I don't know," he said. "And I don't care."

He could feel her annoyance, but courage pushed him toward bravado. "I'll see you later."

When he hung up, he tried to struggle into a heavyweight jacket that had fit him last year but was now impossibly tight all over. The bottom of the closet was deep with dirty white shirts that didn't fit either. On the hook above the mound was the wool lumber shirt he had probably worn for several weeks. The wrist bands were tight, and he rolled them back. He sat on the bed to lace his oxfords, but there was so little string left for the bows that he made knots.

Buses left more frequently from the square toward which he panted. Left over from the age of trolleys was a waiting shed usually filled with uniformed school girls, hugging pyramids of thick books with funny jackets, "Suicide I," "Principles of Arson," "The University of Hard Knocks." But this was midmorning when they were sitting in religion classes, chipping their fingernail polish and practicing their signatures with elaborate designs. Now old ladies in green gabardine coats straddled shopping bags, their thick stockinged ankles dangled below the brown benches. Some of them, he supposed, shortened the day by going to Mass in the rusty red cathedral and then carrying projects around in the bags from nowhere, hopefully to somewhere, then back to nowhere, with crochet hooks and tatting shuttles ready to weave snoods, hats, shawls, christening robes, and laundry bags.

Two of them waddled to the Eden Park bus and sat behind him.

"You going to stay with your grandchildren today, Ag?"

"Yah, while Lynne goes down to the doctor. She's due around Christmas and wants to do some shopping."

"Bet they're cute kids."

"I worry about the little boy, though. He sits out in the back yard and eats all kinds of stuff off the ground—beetles and gum and stones."

"Does he now?"

"I suppose he'll outgrow it and ten years from now be like everybody else."

"Did you know Bird Mahon?"

"Was that Danny Mahon's sister? The one that lived up Redding way and worked in the hat department in Worth's?"

"That's the one. She had such red cheeks when she was a girl."

"She had sugar, didn't she?"

"Yes, that's what she died with. I went to Scully's last night to see her."

"Many there?"

"Nobody. Not a soul. You'd think after all she did for Danny's girls they would have come out of respect."

"They don't go any more. They won't be bothered. How did Bird look?"

"Just wonderful. Her hair waved nice as could be and a beautiful blue dress with a lovely orchid. She was a big woman, you know, but I think it's easier for them when you haven't shriveled up."

During the ride George thought about the myriads of dying and dead that he had not visited and about the children whose personalities were beyond his charting, but then he decided that he did not care about them either. He did not care about José or Maud. Most of all, he did not care about the Morses.

Emily was sitting crying in the living room. For a second George was embarrassed to see her ravaged face without glasses.

"We used to have such good times. I don't know why you got tired of us. We thought about you all the time."

"Why don't you find some other charity case?" he asked.

"What do you mean by that?"

"What I mean is that you've made a profession out of misery hunting. Why don't you find another victim?"

"I don't know how you can be so ungrateful. You were like the family."

"That," he screamed at her, "that is the problem. There are too many families, and who needs more than one?"

He did not look back at her, but went straight out to the movies where he spent the happiest afternoon of the year. He never saw the Morses again.

THE CROOKED

MAN

⮜⧏⧐⮞ The machines in her kitchen bore the brunt of the rage she had never called by name. Natalie slammed the refrigerator door, wore out the faucets by wrenching them too securely shut, ground open cans like a blowtorch, broke a plate or two a week. Still, the effects of struggle were muted; when the afternoon sun slanted across the table and under the sink of the buckled linoleum she might, in spurts, become the housewife, laughing at herself as she washed curtains and windows and put the spice tray in order, but usually she let the cobwebs, crumbs, and plaster dust accumulate.

What her husband, Rev. Donald MacFee, liked was no longer clear. He had approved of too many opposite objects and circumstances to be trusted. Confiding to her that creamed foods made him sick, two days later he ordered finnan haddie, while everyone else was having steak. "You can't trust a word in that damned magazine," he said when *Time* arrived, then based the next Sunday's sermon on a cover story. Was it his memory that was untruthful about the past or was it simply his uncertainty or was it the terrible openness of his

mind? What his mind would look like dissected was her frequent speculation during sermons. Bare—sheer white walls,
iceberg height, reflecting opinions. What was inside an iceberg or a glacier? When the fierce melting reached the center,
would there be left a puddle of foamy lukewarm water or a
steaming clod or dry ice?

When they had been twenty, she convinced herself that his
mind, full of fragrance, was like a dense grove in a Corot painting or a midsummer sketch of Rembrandt with a hut wearing
a fuzzy roof and benches under an arbor where they might
sit. She had assumed that they would spend the first half of
their lives together talking, and when they had said everything, they would be sealed into one self. During their court-
ship eating and sleeping and speaking to others were interruptions in a dialogue marrying them over and over. What
they ate or where they walked was irrelevant. Their tightly
wound need pushed them to days of motion simply to grip
each other in talk. Years later when she had a car, she wondered at the distances they had crossed on foot so indiffer-
ently; the landscape might have been on rollers turning
for them. They would have preferred to scuff over surfaces
that required no notice, through tunnels or hedged mazes or
fog banks or somebody's formal garden. As it was, they
strolled solemnly through the city park under the green statues
of soldiers and reformers until the winter blew them into high-
ceilinged public buildings, museums, theaters, churches, and
post-office lobbies. They moved through the Sunday afternoons heavy in ritual, dutifully visiting exhibits and monuments, but making a serious study only of each other.

"It's just as well that you get to know the man with his

faults," her mother had written on lined paper, flecked with
tomato paste or chili. "I wouldn't want to see you fall into
the pit of misery like I did. Bang, your father walked in with
his sporty ways, never letting on for a minute about his drinking. All I could see was his tattersall cap and jumping out to
open the car door. If I had known how much I'd have to
pay for those manners when I got him home, it would have
been a horse of another color, except that I suppose you
wouldn't have gotten born, of course. What I mean to say is
you don't know when you're well off."

Nor had she known, it seemed, that there are as many ways
to fail in marriage as the people who marry. Never haunted
by obvious poverty and desertion, she discovered the terrors
of goodness and the noisiness of peace.

"It would seem," well-meaning women doing dishes after
Fellowship meetings would say, "that you would have some
children."

"We're waiting until we're more settled. You know, when
he gets a church where we know we'll stay for several years."

Cold, they thought. Who'd want to be married to a minister? All he sees are broken-down marriages and those powdered mice fluttering around the parsonage. The life dries
a man up.

It hadn't really. She could tell them it was far more complex than that. Or she couldn't tell them, because he wouldn't
say. He only made sure there were none. His firm voice shut
the door.

"But why, when you like children?"

"Other people's, not mine."

"You'd get used to them. It happens every day."

"That would be an expensive mistake, wouldn't it? It's not like trying out a new car for a weekend or hanging a painting on a trial basis in the living room."

So on a shelf in the kitchen she kept the birth-control pills with a pencil and a calendar: she drew a line through each day. Her doctor was Cuban; he laughed to fill in the gestures he could not translate. His eyebrows worked over the instruction booklet the day he wrote the prescription.

"One thing, I hear yesterday," he said, his eyebrows sliding across his forehead, "you don't take these one day—you forget one day, and"—slapping his hands together—"just like that, you have baby. You remember that or you be surprise."

It pleased and frightened her to think of the random choice in the fierce waiting of thousands of possible children for the selection of any one to be born. How could one be picked, except thoughtlessly? At any rate, she told herself, I will make him give me a child without his knowing, if not tonight, any one of these nights. The habit of economy was difficult for her to shake; she stood over the garbage pail a long time before lifting the lid and throwing away the jar of pills.

The study door opened, and Donald padded down the stairs in his slipper-sox to stand at the window, looking worriedly at the feeder, which never attracted interesting birds. She knew better than to ask him about his sermon.

"It's almost four o'clock. The afternoon got away from me," he lied. "What are you doing out here?"

"Only trying to pick up. Was I making too much noise?"

"No. Now, don't get defensive. I ask a simple question, and you think it's a condemnation."

"Well, I never know what you like. You look as if almost everything I do is wrong."

"It's my face. I look miserable all the time, I guess."

"You can't much help your face, my mother used to say."

"Your mother says a number of things."

"No, Donald. Let's not start bickering. We sound like all the couples that come to you for help."

"Everything I say to you seems offensive."

"It's my fault. I'm going for a walk into the city. Could you fix yourself some dinner?"

"Sure. Going anywhere in particular?"

"No, just out." She didn't know and was surprised that, feeling like so much stone, she could move quickly once she was outside the house.

It was a restless day. Newspapers and candy wrappers tumbled toward her ankles, and signs and awnings clanged overhead. If she turned her face toward either the store windows or the street, bits of soot blinded her. Their church was an old one. It had been deserted by its congregation for plat houses and now sat among parking lots and TV repair shops.

On the gusty sidewalk were only very old women and their youngest grandchildren, using up the day with long and cheap errands. Amid the cancellation shoe store signs and the Chinese restaurant, she saw a sign for the Belle Isle Gallery, run by someone simply named Gatti, who admitted to no other first or other name. Donald had seen a feature story about Gatti in the Sunday culture section of the newspaper and had invited him to the church coffee house.

"He's the real thing, one gold earring and caustic as crushed glass," Donald had announced. "The kids will love him."

"What will he do when he gets here?" she had wanted to know.

"Nothing. Just be. Let them see what a real artist looks like. Only that. Then they'll have a chance to ask questions. They will want to have a discussion."

"About what?"

"The role of the artist in a free society. What modern art should mean to modern man. The audience he paints for—something like that."

Gatti had come, several hours late, with a young girl in black tights, she giggling: "When I heard this was a church I knew I should wear something black." Donald installed them at a table and tried to present boys and girls, who limply edged toward their dais, but leaned away from their table. Exactly what might awe and attract young people eluded Donald. He kept looking for the Trojan horse, vaccine, lucky number, potion, spell, safe combination, that would unlock their rapture, zip open their hearts so that he might sneak in, dragging God after him. But to Donald they were all Rosetta stones; and well protected inside their leather jackets and long hair, they stared, pitying their minister, this balding blue-eyed kid. They would not exclaim over an artist with an earring. They would not sit in a neat circle around him, soaking up his silence. What they did, instead, was sneak away entirely, slipping like fog out of the cellar, until Donald was forced to see that he was alone with Gatti and his girl.

"Scared them away, preacher," Gatti said. "What did I do wrong?"

"Oh, they're inclined toward restlessness." Donald sighed.

"Sometimes they have to be directed. But they see and remember a lot when they don't seem to be looking, if you follow me."

Gatti smiled meanly over and past Donald's sloping shoulder. "Sure, you're right. Kids see an awful lot."

The dark girl waited, wound up for a signal to leave. When it came imperceptibly, she and Gatti slid to their feet like cats, and the cellar was empty. Gatti had put them on the mailing list for his gallery.

When Natalie saw the Belle Isle sign, she opened the door and climbed a flight of dusty stairs into one sunny room. On the white walls were black periods or exclamation points, amoebae, or stars, or hands clawing at white backgrounds. She waited for her head to connect impressions to words. In the hot room her nose was running, and she was at the same time trying to find a Kleenex, look intelligent, and find some relationship between the title and an angry black sun swooping over some scrawny shrubs. Gatti came from behind a screen.

"Well, the parson's wife pays a call. Wouldn't you like some coffee?"

"Yes, I would, and some explanation, if it's free."

The mugs were thick as cinder blocks. He did not ask her whether she wanted sugar or cream.

"And what brings you to my place of worship? Did the old man send you on an errand? Old man—God—I'll bet I'm ten years older."

"No, I was just walking by and came up to look. What are those all about?"

"Why ask me? You know all about myths. Make up a story

to fit—any story. It doesn't matter if nobody else believes it."

"I'm out of practice."

"What are you people good for anyway if you don't tell myths any more?"

"I really don't know. They keep us for extreme events—for dying and drinking coffee. For unimportant ceremonies on the edges of life. You know, ministers are like palace guards, or firemen or Santa Clauses or morticians."

"Pity those needing instant ceremonies. They remind me of people who are always trying to buy paintings from me by the square foot to match their living room sofas. The kind of people who had bad backs with Kennedy and gallstones with Johnson. You should sell them instant communion, portable faith."

"We're all lazy."

"Some—more. The way I see faith is you should spend all of yourself on it or leave it alone. Me, for instance, I leave it alone. For years God haunted my family."

"How?"

"I wonder what your husband would make of this? My grandmother had vision, or so it seemed. She reported regular chats with a minor saint—one that was out of fashion. So my mother had to top that. For her it had to be a genuine miracle. She was cured of diabetes in a New York chapel by a statue."

"A statue?"

"Oh, you know, I don't mean the statue, but the saint, of course. But can you imagine the situation—how it must have felt, carrying your sandwich bag along Seventh Avenue, settling down to your sewing machine and knowing that a commission was studying your case, all the while you stitched a rack of net evening gowns, took a coffee break, went to a movie, ate your eggplant *parmigian'?* What was it like? Wouldn't that explain why she threw herself at the first unattached male that walked by? She was no beauty and not what you'd call saintly—just a good girl in a navy-blue middy blouse who through some great joke had blundered upon a spiritual signal she wasn't supposed to intercept."

"What finally happened to her?"

"She had ten children, which she must have thought was the best way to barricade herself in and hide from God."

"But all of you must have known about the miracle."

"Naturally, and it was hell on us. All the time she was trying to hide it, the nuns treated us like Moses or the Little Flower. When I played basketball, the team was always asking for one little miracle. I finally turned into a rotten kid. The first time a cop brought me into juvenile court, the judge asked me why I was making God cry."

She said nothing. The night before on the evening news she had watched a young American soldier shoot a North Vietnamese, who grabbed his stomach and entrails before his legs melted. What was one supposed to say? She had given up and would remain silent. Let Donald make up some answers. She would offer a platitude.

"It's a terrible thing either being noticed by God when you don't ask or being neglected when you want attention. I can see how you got to despise anybody in the church."

"Not you. It would be impossible to see you doing anything

significant to be hated for. You were sealed into a kind of paralyzed goodness. You know that, don't you? Neat as a paper clip. Virtue becomes you. It hangs over you like a shroud."

She bent over the cup, which was strong and dark enough to hold truth.

Gatti went on. "I'll tell you how my visions work, and you can despise me for being oracular. That night when I walked into that clerical coffee house, I sized you up instantly. You will live on forever with him, hating him—maybe hating is too strong a word. Let's just say pitying and despising him, like a stomach ache you can't get rid of. You wouldn't ever consider being unfaithful with your body, but your head is something else again. What you do with it, I'm glad he doesn't realize."

He looked carefully at her. If he had been a realistic painter, he might have been memorizing her features to use later. Nervously, she filled the silence.

"We're all a little crooked. That is, anyone who spends any time thinking about the human condition is a little crooked, don't you think?'

"Who's to say who's crooked?"

"What do you mean?"

"Reverend MacFee thinks you are, probably. And I think you are. You think I am—a little. And the people outside on the street and in this building think I am entirely."

"You know, when I was a child, I had a beautiful Mother Goose book, and what I loved best in it was the colored picture of the crooked man in his twisted landscape with the cat with the bent tail and the quaint warped little house. I was looking into it. I never thought there was a crooked woman inside the house. I know Donald so well he's a stranger to me. This is silly to mention, but the other day when I was burning papers in the back yard and throwing the sermon notes out of his wastebasket, I noticed how slanted his handwriting has become, sort of as if it were trying to run away, apologizing over its shoulder—don't notice me. At the end of a line, it becomes just a series of mounds and dots."

Gatti shrugged. Why should he be interested?

She thought of Donald's nervous eyes that ran off the edges of faces and things they were turned toward. Halfway through an important sentence, she saw his eyes drop to the floor or run around the ceiling. No matter what his voice guaranteed in attention, his eyes slid toward the margins. Once in a while, she stood outside his office and knew through the closed door he would be staring at the floor boards under the desk, but not seeing them as the same innocuous FM music boomed through the room.

"So, what are you going to do?" Gatti asked. "You won't leave him."

"No, there isn't any other place to go."

"I'll be blunt with you," Gatti said. "I hate coyness. Did you come here to have an affair?"

"No, you have no idea how lazy I have become too. There wouldn't be enough pleasure to be worth the effort. Among my mistakes was that I admired his locked-up quality. I admired it enough to want to be the same myself. Then I learned that unspent emotion goes stale."

"Some human beings never become used to being human,"
Gatti said. "So, you're waiting around for some new life to
begin?"

Natalie nodded. "I do what I have despised people for doing
before this. I run over the possible horrors that we have
avoided. That's why people take the daily newspaper. To be
superior. To say, we didn't do that. At least we haven't fallen
entirely apart. We didn't get drunk enough to drive the car
into a school bus or become shop-lifters in the meat market
or get multiple sclerosis or gain two hundred pounds. If you
do nothing, you avoid all these. What have you done?" she
asked Gatti impulsively.

"Married, divorced, gone through analysis, admitted I was
only human. Naturally, I started out hoping to exceed the
average, but now I don't even want to leave the flock. It's
warm and easy here. Funny, when I was a kid it was the
artists that were the freaks and now it's the ministers that
wind up being the crooked ones."

"That's true in a way. I suppose you're right," she said, set-
ting down the mug and putting on her gloves. "I guess I'll
go back now to my crooked little house."

At the foot of the stairs she considered the other possible
shelters in which to spend the rest of the afternoon. There
were, of course, the Hawkeses.

"We should," Donald said occasionally, "visit the Hawkeses.
It would be good for us."

"How?"

"They are so good. They're like hot soup or wood fires."

If only one could carry them in the foreground of memory

without having to visit them. Mary Hawkes, wife of the Baptist minister on Maple Boulevard, talked of God as if He were plant supervisor of a company her husband worked for. Mary had the same attitude toward God that wives of service men have toward the Secretary of Defense. The Hawkeses continually referred to "My Jesus" or "Our Lord" and often explained: "You see, God wants us to . . ." Although they could tell in an instant what He wanted, they often scrambled off chairs onto their knees for more direct communication. They did this so rapidly that guests might be taken off guard, Gullivers sitting upright while the Hawkeses were all tidily crouched in corners, their foreheads buried in the chair seats.

Several aspects of the Hawkeses' life were difficult to figure for the stranger, and who wasn't a stranger there? An obvious fertility crowded the house, rising from the pea-green walls, the musty chairs, diapered babies clutching Mary's bosomy frame, the enormous sagging bed in their dark room, the ironing board in the kitchen where she was always steam-cleaning his trousers. Both of them had attended a Southern denominational university named for an evangelist. They loved western programs on TV. They neither smoked nor drank; when the MacFees came for dinner, they served grapefruit juice in cream-cheese glasses on a tray before dinner and smiled smugly. Natalie wondered if they might be hoping to convert Donald.

For children of love, the Hawkeses found an extraordinary number of people who needed to be prayed for before they could be loved. Find the happy man and the Hawkeses' love would feel out his weakness and scratch it into misery. At the same time, they were permanently stunned by other people's humanity. "I can't understand why. Gracious, Danny Flores was in my cub scout troop. That sweet boy couldn't have held up a liquor store. I don't understand," Bob Hawkes lamented.

"We ought," he told the MacFees, "to think about the dead." Beside the church stretched an old graveyard. "Let's walk," he would say, still the troop leader, and they would straggle through the grassy lanes between the slate and brown granite markers, looking at the sleeping white lambs on the smallest stones and the sweet-faced marble maidens hugging flower-decked crosses.

"Weren't they happier, Donald?" he would ask.

"Than whom?" Donald wondered.

Bob waved back over the city. "Oh, than all of us. It is harder to live hopefully now. We try, Mary and me, to be of good cheer, but every day I envy these simple good lives—our grandfather's generation, with so few doubts and temptations."

They scuffed past the clumps of Canterbury bells. Bob stroked a granite sphere to the memory of James Tarbox, Greatly Mourned, 1812-1896. "Remind me to show you when we get back to the study an engraving of this street a century ago: rows of elms and maples, hitching posts in front of all the sturdy handsome houses. The church looked healthier then."

"You mean the Sunoco station and the drive-in hamburg stand weren't here?"

"Yes, but they're only symptoms. Sometimes I do think

we—Mary and me—were born at the wrong time. We like so many things that are old-fashioned."

Natalie could not carry herself to the Hawkeses. She would open their door and send a chill over the green walls. Trudging back to her dark house, she realized that Donald, failing with happiness, had made great friends with misery; it came wet-eyed and leaned its heavy head on his shoulder.

When did I desert happiness, she wondered. She twisted her mind into a knot, remembering childhood. She must have laughed as much as her brothers. She had sat under the kitchen table with a teddy bear on a rag rug that wore a dimmed garden of poppies. The plush around the bear's stitched mouth was worn bald from her kissing. It was a rainy Saturday night, and her mother was greasing the waffle iron. She was happy. They were singing in the assembly hall a scatty tune to which she knew all the lyrics. Then, much later, she and Donald were in a canoe, one second motionless, then securely plowing a neat furrow of dark red water in the cedar swamp at the wildlife preserve. Beneath them tubey stems held the lilies fast to the mud and the fish, like scaly seeds, shot away. They were paddling in utter harmony— stop, spin, stop, glide, better than dancing or eating, talking or loving. They were talking about Schweitzer and imagining that with him in Africa God would be clearer. She had been twenty and happy. Now all faded and diminished in memory.

·   ·   ·

The mailbox was too small and its cover loose. He would not buy another one. When they moved to the permanent parish, new plates, curtains, chairs, doorbell, and mailbox would spring to the fresh walls of the unspoilable life. So the mailman squeezed and bent magazines and letters into the tiny mouth. Today he had not even attempted that but dumped what she already knew was not a very interesting collection of catalogs on the porch floor. Unattractive appeals from leper colonies, Indian ladies' colleges, maimed Korean orphans, lonely merchant seamen, arrived too often to stir any interest or guilt.

Today the pile held the latest alumnae bulletin from her college, forwarded from two previous addresses. And how was the Class of '52 faring? A scatter of photographs in which Violet Ryan, notorious sloth, now wife of a governor, stared from her wing chair beside a Christmas mantel with stockings and several children in red pajamas—"Our five St. Nicks." Among the news notes: "When Helen Fell was named Principal of the Sacket Avenue School, to celebrate she spent the summer earning her M.E. and taking a mule trip in the Grand Canyon." Picture of Helen Fell waving from the lip of the Canyon.

"Melody Hanson and her husband Ray, just promoted to District Sales Manager of Glo-Color, invite any 52'ers passing through Tucson to come calling." It had not been a large class, but Natalie had difficulty remembering any of the graduates who faithfully reported their vacations, children's births, moves, and husbands' promotions. Her friends, the rougher human ones, had melted away, leaving Helen Fell and Melody Hanson, who might have cornered truth after all. Natalie could not even remember the name of her freshman advisor or the sociologists whose brilliant lectures changed her major. Otherwise, she did recall from the faculty a noticeable alcoholic and an ugly section man with a clubfoot who was rumored to give good grades only to girls who accepted his invitations.

The childless have no true measure of time; Natalie would think of herself at one moment as just out of college and in the next as the neat happy wife in a pension plan ad against St. Petersburg palms. She recognized both as lies; she had never been that young, and Donald would forbid her growing that old. They would be stuck in the center of a dead forest when the glaciers came again.

Looking out the window at the side of the door, she thought that possibly the only substance not to be feared was absolute darkness. The region illuminated by the street light was far more sinister than what lay beyond. The lighted city and the lighted house had no comfort for her.

A voice in the living room sorted itself into the latest confession of Mrs. Rose Steinke, who had been enjoying a combination separation-depression. For the first year of her visits Mrs. Steinke had seemed ready to fall apart; with one more miserable day she might decide to murder her alcoholic husband and her stupid lying daughter, and bearing her bloody weapons, would lurch up the parsonage steps exclaiming that she was now free to run away with Donald MacFee. For two years that scene threatened. Before Donald, she had belonged to the AA auxiliary and before that she had slashed her wrists to prove that she was real. Conferences with her were too risky for the study, even with the door open. She came in waves, for a couple of hours daily, then disappeared, either taking herself to another repair shop or learning how to define and describe a new problem. The indestructible veneer under which her miseries lay was at first challenging, then infuriating, finally acceptable as weather.

She had worked up a great crying fit, but even behind the handkerchief her voice was firm and recognizable. "Last night he came in around midnight, stinking. I woke up and bolted the bedroom door, but he shoved it right in. Then he went into Cecile's room and got her out of bed and they went into the kitchen. All I could hear was him singing and something thunking on the kitchen table. So I went out, and Cecile's sitting there in a torn nightie drinking out of the bottle and he's lying all over the table like a dead animal. Oh, hello, Mrs. MacFee. You have a nice walk?"

"Then what did you do, Mrs. Seinke?" Donald asked.

"Poured a dishpan of soapy water on him, the dirty thing, and told Cecile to get into her room, but she put on her coat and went over to her girl friend's house and spent the night. Girl friend! I'd like to see the day she stays with a girl friend. She goes to some house on Division Road. I'm going to find out the number and tell you the next time I come."

Mrs. Steinke considered the horrors of last night with pleasure. "Some family! I haven't spoken to him yet, and no sign of Cecile and I'm so nervous I drop everything. All day spilling change. Anything a customer hands me drops like I was greased. And sweat—did I ever sweat all day, even now, see—feel my hand."

Donald ignored it, but offered instead another day. "You'll come over tomorrow night and tell us how everything is."

"Sure, I will, don't worry. I better be getting back to home, sweet home now. Some sweet home. Not like here."

Donald stood, fondling the doorknob. "Now take care of yourself. We'll see you tomorrow."

When Natalie had washed the dishes and shut off the lights, she went upstairs into the bedroom where he was lying, not reading but watching her with the calm expression she read as sacrifice. Without his telling or even knowing, she accepted the fact that he made love as if it were a purge. I magnify his awkwardness, she thought, and I would do the same with a child, only more.

"No," she said, turning her back on him. "I'm very tired tonight."

"All right," he said. "It doesn't matter to me, really. For some reason I thought you wanted to."

She tried to clutch at one section of the day to hold onto but began discarding all of them as sleep shuffled into the room.

IN UNION

SWEET

❦ "Now Dad, pay attention. Just concentrate for a minute. Try to remember. We need your help."

Would the Pope help the Russians? Would the Christians have helped Pontius Pilate? Ed Killourey squeezed his eyes more tightly and pretended a dry snore, which was going too far. His daughter-in-law Agnes offered to wake him by shouting in his good ear, which she knew annoyed him.

"It's going to be July thirtieth soon again," Agnes encouraged.

Ed opened his eyes to get a good look at the enemy, behind whose bulk her husband Kevin, Ed's blond boy, tried to be a shadow. "Yes, Agnes," Ed said. "For the seventy-five years I've been tearing off the calendar pages, it gets to be July thirtieth about once every year."

For several months he had wondered if they would remember his fiftieth wedding anniversary. Some of the time he wanted to hide any trace of the date he had married May from the Bible or whatever section of their skulls they kept for local and national holidays. The rest of the time he didn't care or was a little attracted by the problem they'd have with the celebration. Playing up his deafness, he overlistened to Agnes calling her cousin, Father Joe Ryan, to get advice she had already decided upon.

"You really think we should try it? He will probably make a fuss when he finds out, but he'd be more offended if we didn't do anything about it, isn't that right? They *all* like attention. The only problem, of course is . . ." Here the voice dropped. They would be discussing May, who couldn't tell the difference between a corn flake and an orchid corsage and who had been under lock and key at the state hospital for the last ten years. Agnes loved all her problems but most of all her crazy mother-in-law. She treasured the suffering trip on the second Sunday of the month to the windy hill-top barracks (so peaceful, such clean air) where the ambulatory senile tormented their visitors with harangues, giggling fits, unblinking silences, and loose tears. Ed never got used to the visits, begged off every other month, and saw no traits in the stranger May had become that encouraged knowing her.

The battle plans had been laid in their bedroom. Ed pressed his forehead to the wall. "We will have to call Dr. Finkel. He's not on duty when we visit, but he will be able to advise, perhaps medicine, a strong tranquilizer, just for the trip down here and the reception. Now, she wasn't bad last week."

Kevin's voice described May wearing a necklace last Sunday made of popcorn.

"But that's just crafts, dear. They make them for therapy. It doesn't mean anything."

Whatever they wanted to call it, Ed knew how great May

was for food. She played with food, hid it, talked about it, must have put away tons of it. Fleshy ropes hung from her shoulders to her elbows. Her thighs were like elephants' rear ends. The cotton dresses issued at Skytop State magnified her size and made more of a stranger of someone who had always been an iron shape under a tight-fitting skirt.

"Just two hours and enough help if anything happens. People understand now." Agnes's favorite bedroom lecture. "Civilized people today all know about mental sickness and talk about it without emotion." Nobody was better at talking about it than Agnes herself. She straightened out Dr. Finkel too. "Mother has become progressively more self-reliant, we think. We feel she will be entirely safe for the afternoon. My husband Kevin and my son Kevin Junior will be constantly at her side. Dr. Finkel, did you by any chance read the article about British out-patient care in the A.M.A. *Journal* for last month? No? Well, I'll Xerox a copy and send it over. Found it in my doctor's waiting room." She was a clipper, a sender of news items, recipes, jokes, cartoons, obituaries. Through every word in the smallest print, she read the newspaper as if it were an ammunition dump or something to make soup of.

"What we have in mind, Dr. Finkel, is a very simple reception. No strain at all, just a few old friends."

What old friends, Ed wondered. The milkman, the insurance agent, the boy selling magazine subscriptions, the Fuller Brush man, the two or three fearless fighting ladies in full battle corset who marched up the front steps to collect for cancer or the Animal Rescue League?

"We don't have much family, you know. My cousin
Father Ryan, of course, and we'll have to ask Kevin's sister,
the one that never comes to the hospital. These affairs mean
more to them than we realize. Right, Dr. Finkel. Your parents and mine weren't this lucky."

Ed clicked his teeth. It was hard to keep still. He was
often surprised to watch his feet tapping to a tune he
couldn't hear. The ends of his body seemed to be outposts,
poorly connected with the center, and the outposts were
getting more rebellious every week. Stuffed into shoes, his
feet were sometimes stones, and thresholds might have been
mountains or trenches. A reception would mean dressing
up and trying to stand straight and talking to a lot of people
that soured your stomach.

"Right, Dr. Finkel, that's just what we thought. It
would do them good. Oh dear, no, we don't expect any im-
provement. Goodness, no, we don't believe in miracles.
We're more enlightened than that."

Why such humility? With concentration, she just might
bring one off. Years ago, he had taken May on a terrible trip
to a shrine, which he had tried to forget all about. He had
once been a believer, but not Agnes. Even if a miracle struck
her dead, she would try to reason with it.

"Oh certainly, Dr. Finkel. She'll be back before the first
sign of tiredness. So glad you see it our way."

Agnes advanced, demolishing opposition like a shy tank,
Kevin safely hidden behind. Her tone was the same for any
subject—termites, cancer, hairpins, atomic bombs, spumoni.
"Now Dad, July thirtieth is your fiftieth wedding anniver-

sary, and we're planning a little party for the Sunday before
that. We wondered if you could help us a little? There must
have been some attendants—people who stood up for you?"
Agnes often translated words she assumed were too complex
for him so carefully that he could look into her fuzzy mouth
at her pale gums.

"Dad, now pay attention for just a minute. You must
have had a bridesmaid and a best man? Could we get them
here?"

"Let's see—" pretending to grope. "Yes, there was a best
man. Name of Tom Haxton. Yes, that's right."

"Well, where is he, Dad?" They waited respectfully.

"I don't know," he said. Which was a lie, of course. He
often passed Tom Haxton's stone in Old St. Mary's, dead two
years after the wedding, with the flu. He had even gone down
to the railroad station for Tom's mother to collect the pine
box when it was shipped from Fort Dix. When the train arrived, Red Cross men scrambled into the baggage room with
five boxes, each stenciled in black letters with a name and
instructions not to open.

"Well, I guess we'll have to put our thinking caps on to
figure out where Mr. Haxton is. And, Dad, what are we going
to do about Theresa?"

Next to her mother-in-law, Theresa was Agnes's favorite
topic, the black sheep sister-in-law. They would always bring
her up like undigested food. Mostly with indirect comments
—live and let live, takes all kinds, none of us are perfect. The
whole point was Theresa had escaped the nest and Kevin
hadn't, so Theresa was the black sheep. Ed knew she was

no better than she ought to be. Fight, fight, it was all the time she was around. Sulky, whiny, grateful as an adder, she was always calling attention to herself. The Holy Name usher coming up to him at Mass: "I don't like telling you this, Mr. Killourey, but that girl of yours is always going in the boys' side of the church. Twice we had to drag her out of a pew full of boys." And the sisters coming up to him in the grocery store: "She could be a bright girl, but she's so high-strung." Blazing cheeks, hair all over her face, panting and racing along the pavement, feet like horses', she did not look like anyone in their families, nor like anyone who lived near them. He used to wonder about it. He'd heard tell of a dope fiend nurse who worked in the baby ward at St. Joseph's that used to bring the wrong ones for feeding. And everybody on Quarry Hill knew Danny Donan couldn't have a child, but his wife had five and they all looked like the Syrian fruit peddler who came on Tuesdays. They tried to treat Theresa as if she belonged, but she kept saying, "I'm leaving this dump as soon as I make the fare," although May tried to wash her mouth out with soap. She packed herself and all her queer notions —that macaroni would turn into snakes in her stomach, that her uncle was on a "Wanted" poster in the post office— and took off for Chicago where she was supposed to be some kind of hairdresser. Some hairdresser, Ed guessed.

"I don't see what Theresa has to do with this," he told Agnes and Kevin, who squeezed their lips and went back to the bedroom to cope. In their guarded comments the house tensed.

Agnes's voice marched on behind the partition: "We'll

have to serve sandwiches, but it's between meals so no one can expect much. That's the whole point of three o'clock in the afternoon. And a half-inch gold stripe on all the cups, plates, and napkins. Paper, of course."

Agnes was wearing out her stomach and head over the party. She perspired until great dark circles stained the armpits of her dress down to the waist. "No, we want flowers in season. And make sure the centerpiece doesn't get there before three. I don't want it wilted."

"You put my boss's son on the list, didn't you?" Kevin learned fast.

"Of course. But you can't have the Sheas. He married Alice Tobin's sister, and after Mrs. Tobin didn't leave them anything, they don't speak. We need the Tobins more."

The party became a battle to be prepared against sabotage. "If she gets out of hand, Kevin and little Kevin will take her to the car." Little Kevin—175 pounds of solid beef behind the ears. "If Father Ryan has had a little too much to drink, no speeches from anyone. If Catherine Meech begins to cry herself sick, try to play the music louder and drown her out."

For music she found a harmonica, an accordion, and an electric guitar. They could drown out Niagara. They were so loud you couldn't hear them, which was just as well.

"So the trouble begins at three," Ed said the morning of the party, but no one answered. It was raining, although Agnes would not admit it. "It's clearing, going to be fine." She had taken the best weather report from somewhere— twenty years back or from clumped tea leaves. While the wind blew doors shut and sucked them open again and pushed the heavy branches toward the ground, Ed hoped for floods to block the roads and force them to ride the rooftops.

But it merely drizzled, and Agnes reassured the callers: "Oh, no, we wouldn't think of canceling for a little rain. It'll clear. You wait and see. Just to be sure, we've moved the chairs indoors. Oh, he's looking forward to it. We all are."

Women in large hats carried cakes into the kitchen. Mustard, the cat, in the midst of a depressed life, sensed a major threat, dug her claws into a tree, realized that no gesture could hold back the tide of change, sat on the maple tree's lowest limb, paws muffed beneath her scorning face. Behind the closed door of his room, Ed wished that Tom Haxton had lived. Tom would be only seventy-one and able to take him away.

Agnes tried to attract his attention by talking loudly outside the door. "You're sure, Dad, you don't want to drive out to Skytop. Nothing needs to be done around here. I'd love to go, but I promised to be at the hall before the flowers." She said she had hired the Spanish-American post because it was more convenient, whatever that meant, but Ed was sure it was simply cheaper.

"No," he shouted through the door. "I'm not going. I haven't read the Sunday papers yet." That shut her up.

"Well, I suppose the Columbas can pick you up. They're such kind people." Meaning he was not.

The Kevins (Ed had long ago started to think of them as brothers in some TV daytime serial) put on their madras jackets and their after-shave lotion and went over the hills to fetch May. Agnes was ready an hour later for public display, six inches of glittering tapestry above her carved hair, preserved from the damp by a shell of hair spray, an acre of some thin pink cloth draped and tucked in grand shape, and see-through shoes. What to see, Ed asked himself, but bunions, corns, calluses, and wide and aching size 8's?

"The Columbas will be here at two-thirty." She meant he should stand in the picture window aimed at the curb. "You'll lock the door and won't let Mustard in. I'm sure the Columbas know the way, but you remember, it's the Spanish-American Post, Roosevelt Avenue, Spanish-American Post . . ."

"Yes, you told me several times." Twenty, to be exact. It was a wonder she did not write the address on a piece of paper and pin it to his coat.

How would it be if he ran away? He could send smoke signals, if anyone cared, but no one did. He was seldom left alone in their house. What would happen if he crushed the Belleek and threw the Waterford vase out the picture window, robbed Agnes's budget bank, and took off? But in the next half hour they would find him behind someone's hedge or sneaking along the freeway. By never referring to the day Dad misbehaved, Agnes would make it a measure of time like 1492 or 1775. It was not worth handing her such a trump card, so he stood docilely as if the living room were a bus stop until the Columbas' sudden red microbus bounced into its loading space.

There were seven or eight Columbas. Ed could never remember how many or their names or which ones were the parents. They were all dark, worried, and a little hunched from perching in the bus, the youngest often eating and sleeping there.

"Well, here we are, Mr. Killourey," an older voice—it must have been Betty Columba's—said. "We never seem to stop for breath, do we? When Francis's teacher asked her to draw a picture of home, she drew a red bus. Was I ever embarrassed. But, as Joe says, a few years more and one of them is bound to have a driver's license. Then this chauffeur will retire. Take your time, Mr. Killourey. That's a high step. Clara, you get in the back seat. I don't know where. Anywhere. If Nicky won't shove over, sit on top of him."

The microbus lurched along, reminding Ed of a Model A he had once and before that a buggy.

One of the youngest Columbas wanted to know: "Is there going to be a wedding?"

"No, once there was, a long time ago," another answered.

"Who's he going to marry?"

"He's already married, dope."

"Where's his wife, then?"

"We're going to see her later," Betty Columba told them.

Nobody belonged to lodges and orders much any more. Ed was a life Elk but never went to meetings. Who would be there? Did he want to grow old with the Odd Fellows or spend retirement with the Woodmen of America or be buried in a Grange Memorial Service—ten or twelve old people held together with big wrinkled purple sashes?

The Spanish-American War Post had been the home of

a railroad president who killed himself in the basement forty years before. It was set back from Roosevelt Avenue in a park of its own which was strangely tropical; thick bushes with wide leaves seemed to give off heat; between the dense green grass the soil was black. Very old wisteria vines hid the porch and darkened the long windows of the first floor. No gathering or army could fill the house.

"Well, this is your great day, Mr. Killourey." Some smiling fool with an umbrella at the door of the microbus grabbed his arm and pulled him, boom, down to the sidewalk. "Easy now. Can't let you slip on these wet bricks."

Someday, Ed thought, I will bite one of them. Get down on all fours and bite an ankle, right through the sock. But he could see the headlines—Elderly Man Caught after Mid-Town Pursuit. Bites policeman, usher, bus driver, parking lot attendant. Committed for observation.

They steered him into the great hall, bordered with blue-cushioned folding chairs from the nearest funeral parlor. Up front on the table with the centerpiece and the open guest book was a make-believe gold tree with bills squeezed to make leaves. Ed squinted at a photograph of two people inside a gilt frame. "Nice-looking couple, weren't they?" Betty Columba asked, standing beside him, weighted down on each arm with a baby like a shopping bag.

"I can't get close enough to see who they are," Ed answered. He refused to cry over an old picture of two clowns in their fancy duds. The faces of the women turned angrily away from him; he was not playing fair. Being feeble was permitted, but not disowning the past.

"I think I'll sit down," he muttered, and all the people standing around made a path for him as if he were contagious. The men looked at their shoes; the women made comforting noises; the children whispered and sucked their fingers or giggled. When Ed moved quickly, the landscape slid as if it were a theater curtain sliding shut. There was also a sound inside his head, difficult to explain what it was exactly, a spring flood running through a sluice gate or a squeaky hinge on a cellar door. It used to trouble him only when he moved his head. Now, bolder, it had moved in permanently, even waking him at night. Speaking past it was like pushing through fog or cotton candy or swimming out of weed or lily pads.

The active boy in the red jacket holding his harmonica was making faces at Ed. No, not faces. Words. Damn the sound in his head. It was too strong to hear the boy's thin mumble. Everyone he knew mumbled, was it on purpose? Favorite song? Whose? Mine? Nothing you'd be likely to know, that's the truth. Hoped that would squelch red jacket. Never did like music much, a faraway catchy tune out of doors in the summer, a band concert full of steam, clang, and toot, everyone knowing it was only to stretch your legs to or to make talk easier, but he could never tell one song from another.

The woman with the accordion hanging over her stomach was whispering to red jacket, and they decided on some slidy combination to keep them busy and the crepe-paper bells swirling. A stream of antlike women carried trays back and forth, the same tray, probably, making work for themselves. All around the porch of the house the thick bodies of men clustered. Ed supposed that was where he should be standing rather than among women opening their pocketbooks and staring into them as if they were full of marvelous jewels rather than old Kleenexes and bent toothpicks. But the effort of lifting himself out of the chair and lurching toward the porch was too much, so he sat among the women, his hand over his eyes as if he were dozing. "He's asleep," they told the children and the musicians, and then turning to each other: "They get tired, you know. It's remarkable, though, how they manage." The whole world was made up of the they's and the we's. He was, of course, one of the they's. Over his head floated stories about our children, our mortgages, our bad backs, our summers. Between some of the men's shoulders Ed looked at the trees, a lush green over their stark black trunks. Even through the veil of rain the maples were fierce.

Staving off the terrible moment, they might all have been waiting for a barium test, a tax audit, the principal's decision, or confession. They saw all chance of flight sucked away by the clock. The accordionist turned sharply from the window, nodded, and the guitar player stood against emergency.

Young Kevin in businesslike trot came round the bend, happy as Elliot Ness. "They want you now. You have to go out and help." Is this what it mean to be seventy-five, to be ordered around by a half-baked bellboy with as much respect as a canary, and, saddest of all, to have everyone know he was your grandson?

But Ed marched out to the car and a sorry sight—Kevin

and Agnes coaxing May, or the stranger they called May, out
of the car. He supposed to anyone who hadn't seen her ever
before she might look normal, if they had bad eyes or if they
looked at her from the side or the back. There was something
about their eyes and the smell of their clothes. On tranquilizers she lumbered around like a freshly fed cobra.

"Hello, May," he said, not offering to tug her out of the
front seat.

"Hello," she said, not looking, except at a plastic Holy
Family group on the dashboard.

"See, here's your corsage, Mother," Agnes said. The corsage could be dangerous. He could see that she was trying to
figure out whether it was a salad or a puzzle to be unscram-
bled.

"I want to go back home. Take me home now." She regarded the hill as home. He had heard her on this topic before. The cries would mount.

"In a little while you'll go home. There are some nice people inside that want to meet you. There is going to be a party.
Look who's here. This was your bridesmaid fifty years ago
Monday. Remember?" Who could find any familiar curve in
the skull peering into the car?

Ed had thought he could put an end to the foolish business by turning and running away. At least during the morning he had promised himself that he could march off the
premises with some grand insult. Looking down at May,
he realized how thin her gray hair was and noticed her tight
hands grasping her knees in fear.

The bridesmaid, May, and he were the only ones left who

had stood in the back yard that morning in their stiff collars and leg-of-mutton sleeves and run to catch the trolley down near the car barn with valises and parasols and rice flying.

"May," he suddenly asked, "do you remember how Tom Haxton caught your bouquet? Came sneaking in when you were throwing it and stole it away from the girls?"

She looked interested. "He was a handsome fellow. Whatever became of him?"

"I don't know," he lied again. "But you were a good-looking bride yourself. There's a picture inside that you ought to see."

She got out of the car and scuffed onto the veranda, and with the accordion and the guitar making a great racket, she was led toward the centerpiece, the nut dishes, the candles, the crepe-paper bells, and the photograph, which meant as little to her as it had to Ed. She looked grouchily at all the helpful women who repeated: "This is your cake. This is a centerpiece made of roses. These are candles. This is your wedding picture. Isn't that nice?" The word "nice" was catching; husbands and children used it freely. Father Joe used it in his short speech about what the occasion could teach everyone. Women shoving cookies and ice cream at the guests used it. Ed and May did not say anything. They pretended to read a long telegram from Theresa, but the print was too small to see. May did not eat her corsage or tear apart the money tree. Ed did not try to run away. Agnes circled the room, whispering to her friends: "They're being so good, aren't they? Everything is so nice, isn't it?"

Through the window Ed looked at the parking lot where,

inside a pink station wagon, a German shepherd prowled against each streaked window; exiled for bad behavior into his blue Chevrolet, the Cronins' four-year-old son strained to release the hand brake. When he succeeded, the car rolled down the grassy lawn and thudded smartly into the Suplickis' brightly polished Oldsmobile.

The hall emptied. John Cronin and Bill Suplicki began to scream at each other.

"My God, look at what your fool kid did."

"What were you doing, parking in that crazy place?"

"That kid belongs in the Don Bosco Shelter. One night you'll wake up and he'll be standing over you with a butcher knife in his hand."

"I'll sue you. One more word and I'll sue you."

"A criminal. That boy will grow up and be an assassin."

John Cronin hit Bill Suplicki on the shoulder. He had been aiming at the cheek. Ed could see that they did not know how to fight, but their wives and the other men took them seriously and held them apart like tigers.

May turned away from the window. "What is it all about?" she asked Ed.

"A fight. Just two men fighting about the car."

"No. I know that. But what it is really all about?"

He shook his head. How could he answer? It was far too complex, and he didn't know either. For once in his life he was almost glad to see Agnes bustle into a room.

"Time to go home, Mother. Haven't we had a nice day?"

THE OLD

GARDENER'S

DAUGHTER-IN-LAW

The ward held twenty men. It was on the second floor of a grotesque fieldstone and iron mass left over from the TB era. Disused porches beyond the windows were darkened by rusted fire escapes.

Ann Devaney carried a basket of old magazines, some hard candy, and five polished apples. Sometimes it was pears or chocolate pudding in a plastic container. During the week she gathered offerings unthinkingly until there seemed to be enough to fill the basket and then to spread over the bed tray. Her husband, Phil, had been in this hospital only six months, but already she could not remember Sundays that did not include an early dinner, picking up ancient Mrs. Di-Biasi, whose husband, a stroke victim, had been on the first floor for two years, and driving sixty miles toward this rusty castle, the radio turned to the same Methodist hymn service against Mrs. DiBiasi's discussions of enemas and catheters.

"Hi, dear." She leaned over his thin chest and kissed his dry lips. He smelled of nothing. She always expected faint camphor or pill coating or sour stomach, but his lips were a tasteless bleached terry-cloth line.

His right thumb tried to grasp her sleeve, fluttered once or twice and gave up. "Pretty hat. Have I seen that before?"

"About a hundred times," she whispered into his ear.

"How's Francie?"

"Fine. She'll be up one of these Sundays, but it's Jim all the time. I don't know what to do."

Ann had always known what to do since she gave up crawling for two feet, and the more certain she became, the more she practiced indecision for his benefit, but Phil seldom rose to the bait. His eyes watered slightly. "What's it to me? For ten years I couldn't do her any good. The best thing would be for her to get married and forget our troubles."

"Oh, she wouldn't make a move without your advice."

Ann could see she'd carried the game too far. He was silent, staring toward his feet. His body lay perfectly outlined beneath the thin covers. When she glanced over his tense knees, his eyes trapped hers. There were so few places to look in the limited space, she had to control her face constantly. Certain anecdotes distracted. "Bill Stafford asked for you this week. His boy had three toes sliced off by a power mower. Slipped on the grass and his foot went under." His illness had inoculated Phil against other misery. He was part of the underworld of the sick and helpless. "He was at Wayland General and had Dr. Hodosh, the same one you had over there."

"He's a good man."

"The best." They had agreed on this several dozen times. The hospital Mafia was a safe topic. Where the doctors spent their vacations, where their children went to college, what kind of cars they drove, what problems their wives had.

"Do anything interesting this week?" he asked.

The first years of being in hospitals off and on, they had clutched each other silently during visiting hours, trying to protect each other against fear and making it so bad and deep their teeth chattered. But now that her life had become a kind of scrapbook, she found anecdotes to put on the tray beside the fruit and magazines.

"You know, Father Nadeau's on vacation. We had this substitute from the Marists who gave a sermon everybody's been talking about on glowing after the Last Judgment. He said we each would have a different glow, and he was sure that we wouldn't want our neighbors to see what skimpy glows we would give off. After that the kids were calling him Father Firefly."

He smiled. "I wonder how many watts my soul has? Or maybe some would be like sparklers and just sizzle a while before they gave out. Now, Dad would be a comet. How is he?"

Ann and Francie lived with Phil's widowed father, David, who was a gardener and worked for the city. "He'll be up on Wednesday. He's been working like crazy the last couple of weeks. Moving all the delicate plants indoors and transplanting the mums. They're going to have a display this year that would knock your eyes out. About a thousand more rust and orange ones. I forget how it's supposed to look. He'll tell you about every bud on Wednesday." She knew perfectly how it would look, but she had to save a half-hour's talk for Dave when he came. "I went one day to the park, you know, to look at the roses. I mean, he asked me so many times. So I went."

Phil looked toward the gray sky. "Last week I saw a kite out there, a big Japanese dragon."

"That must have been nice," she said, making up her picture of the kite.

"The grounds patrol got them to take it down. This is all state property. Nobody's supposed to fly kites here."

"I guess there must be a reason."

Unlike Phil's other hospitals, this one was all business; even eating was a marginal activity, lasting about twenty frenzied minutes three times a day before all signs were erased. It was so bare and well-built that no one could scratch or dent a surface. It was sterilized and washed until it looked dirty, but had merely faded. During the week an army of grounds men pruned and worried over individual trees in the great park. They painted cheery signs: "Happy Easter!" "Joyous Noel!" They built benches and tables upon which no one took his ease. They planned vistas and groves too remote for any patients to focus upon. Or if they did, they were past caring. Year round, the sun slanted weakly through the heavy pines onto the massy walls and the heavy roofs. Spongy moss and grand rhododendron spread richly.

"Could I fix your pillows?" He shook his head. Only the nurses could make him comfortable now. The Devaneys had become gentle but shy with each other. In their long silences, while she sat on the edge of the plastic chair beside him and he stared over the heaped-up bed tray, the radiator buzzed, and her mind drifted. They never fought. They had nothing to fight over. This distant burden, this clean and drying body on the bed, had become child, brother, father, stranger, and lover in her head's confusion. She was embarrassed to be strong and healthy. Recently the medicine cabinet door had swung open while she was taking a bath, and she saw unexpectedly reflected there her firm body beneath the half-frown she wore like a wedding ring. No rounding her shoulders and throwing out her stomach would reduce that effect. And what use was it? Francie was a dumpy girl given to two chins already and devising hairdos that would draw attention to her eyes. She wore contact lenses at night and spent a lot of money on her teeth.

"Mrs. DiBiasi come with you today?" Phil asked.

"Oh, yes." She hadn't missed a Sunday for two years. "He has a sore on his cheek that they're cauterizing."

"The night nurse told me that he's really fading."

"I guess that's right. He's on oxygen now." Most of the time, his eyes were shut, and he repeated the name of his son, never a particular favorite, who lived in Detroit and never visited. Mrs. DiBiasi drew conclusions from the way he breathed and the color of his eyelids. The doctors listened to her. She brought minestrone soup in a Thermos and drank it herself.

A dark man neither of them knew stood at the foot of Phil's bed. "How's it going, fella?" He shook the rail at the bottom of the bed.

"Can't complain," Phil replied.

Some people who came to visit relatives found themselves better off with strangers. They boomed greetings through doorways and told old and safe jokes to men in other wards. The others are dying, they thought, the others, not mine. I am visiting the others.

"Nice view you have here, fella," the stranger said, then leaned closer to Ann. "You'd better watch out for your husband with that new charge nurse. Cutest little thing you ever saw." On his way to the next bed he winked at Phil.

Waiting keeps some people young, Ann thought. Trees grow rings every year, and the women in her office had all kinds of measures: the summer we went to Yosemite or the year we moved to Red Chimney Road. Listening to the women talk of vacations, movings, promotions, mortgage payments, and early retirement, she felt a widow or single.

At the end of the afternoon, Phil told her when it was time to go so that she would not have to stare at her watch and make up the excuses for leaving—the lights, the weekend traffic, the washing. "Love," he whispered when she kissed his cheek, but his voice was so faint that it might have been some other half-said word. From the door she waved again. He was already trying to open a magazine, and she did not look but fled down the stairs to collect Mrs. DiBiasi.

There was a tangle of tubes around the old man's bed. Under the crinkle of the oxygen tent, his yellow face swam, the mouth calling hoarsely for the indifferent son. An anti-congestion machine waited to clear his throat, and the machines and pills canceled each other: digitalis and tranquilizers, iron extract and anticoagulant, vitamins and bromide. For all to see, his urine dripped, his chest labored, his heart shuddered, and his blood trickled. He could hold back no secret part of himself. Ann and Mrs. DiBiasi walked sturdily out of the large reception hall toward the parking lot as if they had attended some public ritual.

All the way home, Mrs. DiBiasi, who loved to talk on the way to the hospital, was silent. Ann listened to a football game. Driving out the heavy stone gates with the state seal, they might have been two women who had just left their sons at the training school or their daughters at the prison farm. The prison visiting rooms had screens, but in many ways the prison was a more hopeful place.

How her mind was slipping out of control troubled Ann terribly. Her head fixed on objects and people independently. It behaved like a moth, sitting on the edge of a leaf, flapping its wings. On a bus a few months ago she found, staring at a photograph opposite her seat, that her eyes had walked down the road in the photograph and turned a corner that wasn't in the photograph and that she was advancing toward a brick wall at a perilous rate. Sometimes in church or waiting in line at the supermarket, she discovered her careless eyes consuming a face near hers, eating it to the bone. Anyone noticing such intensity turned away angrily, believing that his skin had been violated. Touching the catsup bottle in her kitchen or handing the fried egg to Francie, she moved into a bright dream.

"Mother," Francie said. "Mother. You must be a million miles away. I just told you that I think we're going to be engaged." Francie pointed happily at a spot on a decorative towel tacked to the wall. It was a cloth calendar for the whole year, surrounded by roses and birds. "Right in there, in March, we could get married."

"Why not," Ann replied, knowing that her voice was all wrong for the occasion. "I mean, any time you and Jim see fit."

"I wish you'd pay attention to Jim. He thinks you don't like him."

"I was trying to leave you alone. I thought you wanted to be alone."

"We're going to drive out to see Dad next weekend. You won't have to go. I mean, it's a hard trip every Sunday. You never get a chance to rest."

Did Francie know that some Sundays if it weren't for Mrs. DiBiasi she would turn around at the city limits and telephone in some message? What would all of them think if they knew how easily she could forget—or really had forgotten—Phil? If they knew how dangerous her mind had become, they might lock her up at night. This neat woman who lined her bureau drawers with scented paper and kept her gloves in plastic boxes was trying to hide the horrors in her head. Who thought that these were easy years? She envied lumpy Mrs. DiBiasi, fifty years married. At her age, Ann thought, she would be crazy or waking up in seedy motel rooms alone with an empty whisky bottle and no memory of how she got there. The surface health got thinner daily. Her father-in-law was no longer safe in his own house, and he showed signs of knowing it, too.

With Francie out so many summer nights, she and David sat in the kitchen talking over coffee. "I talk too much because other people are too quiet," he said, spreading his lips tightly. She was alarmed by his confidences but more afraid of his silences. On Sundays, he washed his own clothes, his underwear and shirts, while he smoked a cigar or two. He would probably have done all the laundry in the house, and well, too, if she had not hidden her things and Francie's in closet bags.

He was always bringing home flowers. When she walked into the kitchen after letting off Mrs. DiBiasi, he had the sink full of asters.

"This is the last of them," he said. "I thought we might as well look at them."

"They're a sad flower, aren't they?" She held a tough purple head. "To look at this one you'd think he'd outlast all the frosts and sleet of three winters."

"It's the stems that give out. Right up near the heads, but they keep on blooming like fools."

"That's a pretty vase." Ann touched its lacquered red and green leaves. Sometimes when he brought flowers, he let her arrange them, but the next morning she would discover that he had shifted them to a better vase.

"I bought that one in California the year we drove across the country, before Phil was born. Theresa never liked it. She wanted smooth finish on things. Poor Theresa, I sometimes think of how she used to show me pictures of rooms in some magazine and say oh how I'd love to have that room, and I'd say maybe you'd like to own a few things in that room. But she'd shake her head and say, no I want the identical same room."

"It would have been like living in the model rooms on the second floor of Turabian's Furniture Store." Ann could see the well-corseted prow of her mother-in-law advancing through the lamps and end tables and stately divans in Turabian's cutaway home for moderns.

"It's a good thing we were too poor for that. It has its advantages. Once in a while I had the chance to earn good money, but escaped just in time." Dave laughed. "Just as well. It all comes to the same. Theresa thought I should have gone to work for the helicopter plant in the war. She moped around here hardly speaking for a couple months then. You know, it got so bad I took to sleeping in the potting shed. I felt so damned guilty about not doing what she wanted."

He often brought up the months in the potting shed until Ann imagined him taking off his glasses and putting them with his watch on a safe shelf and stretching out under a coarse blanket among the trays of seedlings and clumps of pots. This had been his major act of disobedience.

"You wouldn't have liked the factory." She always said that.

"I suppose, but it wouldn't have hurt me to give in that once. It always bothered her that I was a gardener. It didn't seem right for a man. Her father was a miner, and that was all right. She got nervous when I brought flowers into the house. She probably didn't do it on purpose, but Christmas she'd buy one of those aluminum trees, and in the center of the dining room table she left a bouquet of cloth daisies. Said she hated the mess of the real ones, the dirty water and the stinky stems. Maybe they did give her headaches. We all have our ways."

He used statements like this to bring down the curtain of the past for a while. Now he would offer her milk and a sandwich and have a bowl of cold cereal himself and get ready for bed. "Why don't you take this onto the porch and have a look at the paper. There won't be many more days you can sit out there."

It was his house and his right to tell her to eat the sandwich and read the *Gazette*. She turned the pages, glancing at other people's troubles. DeGaulle has foot fungus, Swedes drive on the right, the Pope cautions speeders, bank robber kills for two hundred dollars in coins. If she stopped reading for a year, the same events would have occurred when she began reading again. The flowers inside the house told what season it was, and needed no help from her to bloom at the right times. Her back ached, and no position in any chair in the house would ease it. There was nothing to do but to go to bed. Francie was probably now rearranging her hair in the front seat of Jim's car and trying to distract him with talk about the wedding and the bridesmaids. Francie could take care of herself.

Letting all the doors close loudly enough for him to know where she was, Ann called out to David: "Good night. I'm going up now."

He answered from the front of the house: " 'Night, Ann. I'll put the milk bottles out. You sleep well."

She climbed the stairs in one brittle posture. Shutting her

bedroom door, she leaned against it without putting on the lights. Through the window straight across the quiet street was the Esso station where plastic pennants flapped and rattled, and inside the lighted garage office the proprietor sat, feet up on the desk. She and Phil had come back to this house and his old room when he could hardly walk. At first he crawled up the stairs by grabbing the steps above him and pulling himself slowly up while she and David went loudly into the kitchen to do the dishes. Finally, David stayed behind while she waited in the kitchen without drawing a breath. One night she had seen David straining, half pulling and pushing Phil's knees up, at the same time holding him by the belt against falling. Later she and David had linked hands over Phil's thin back and pulled him toward the bedroom door. Then David had dragged him toward the bed, where he crouched, his yellow face drawn toward his groaning mouth from which great breaths came.

Until they had bought a cot, she had slept carefully on the edge of their big bed. There was not one spot of his body where he could stand to be touched. In the nights when she couldn't sleep, not daring to move, she rested on her back staring at the patterns the leaves made on the ceiling like sharp-feathered birds. That was just over a year ago. One night when Phil was deeper than usual under the sleeping tablet and on his side, she had slowly felt his body through the thin pajama bottoms, not in the accidental touch of helping him dress, but exploring a wrecked world. Her hands rested on his cold buttocks. They were pricked with tiny rough spots, and the long bones stuck out in rounded points.

He had given up getting dressed then and sat around the house in one of Dave's old bathrobes. For Christmas Day she had helped him put on his blue suit so that he could be dressed for dinner. He made out the tags for Francie's gifts with a stiff hand, taking a half hour to get them right, resting his fingers after every stroke. His father had done Phil's shopping and had bought a housecoat for her. "He used to buy Mom's clothes. He has good taste, doesn't he?" It was a dark-blue corduroy and fit perfectly. She was embarrassed to wear it after Phil left for the hospital and was always dressed when she went downstairs to fix breakfast. She and Dave had worked out a perfect schedule that allowed her to be frying the eggs while he shaved and her to be using the bathroom when he ate.

Ann undressed in the dark. Even at that, she caught herself in old habits, putting the nightgown over her shoulders, pulling the slip straps down and wriggling out of the slip like a fish, never showing her body to the dark. Twenty years ago in their bedroom in Akron, Phil had laughed. "That's the damnedest way to take off your underwear. Are you afraid I'll see your warts, or is it feathers?" He lifted her nightdress, and the next morning she wondered if the Bergsons across the street could have seen in at the edges of the window shades.

Every night the myth of Phil coming home blew away again. In the summer she had once driven down with David on a Wednesday, and found the doctor who was responsible for the floor. You weren't supposed to ask questions of the staff, but what difference did it make now?

"What can I say, Mrs. Devaney?" the doctor answered. "Who knows? He could have another arrest. Most likely he'll get a lot weaker though. After we finish with him here—just between us—you should be looking around for some long-term convalescent hospital. We have a list to help you. It's what I'd call a long-term thing. A little breakdown here and another there. You know what I mean, body functions going all the time. And finally, maybe a blessing, you know what I mean, his mind giving out. But then again, it may not follow that course. Every one of us is a separate case, isn't that so?"

In the summer she had taken sleeping tablets, but they had deadened the nights so blackly that she abandoned them. Better to toss on a real bed into fifty or a hundred cramped spots, knowing that it was your own body doing the tossing. On this same bed she had said good-bye to Phil's poor bones. Probably this was the same bed he had gotten up from twenty years ago and driven over to Riverpoint where she had been visiting cousins. Walking back to the cousins' house from the movies with him on the second night they were alone, she trembled so much that she couldn't talk. At the end of the week when he said, "I can't be long-winded. If you'll marry me, I'd be awfully happy," she had said, "thank God!" because that was what she meant. Now the bridegroom had shrunken to the yellow frame she thought of as a child or father lying in the distant ward.

She had cried twice, once about ten years ago when the doctors had told her after the first numb spot on his right foot what the disease was and then again when Phil's clawed hands could not grasp a fork, and he had begun, behind her back, to lap his plate like a dog. That time she had simply turned away and run up the back stairs and then up still another flight into the attic where she stuffed the hem of her skirt into her mouth to keep from being heard. Bent over their dusty furniture, stored in Dave's attic until they had another place, she cried away an hour. When she came down, Phil was in bed again, and Francie was doing her homework at the kitchen table.

"Gramps went out after we did the dishes."

Where did he go those first years they all lived together? Before they darkened the house with their thick miseries, the place had been his refuge. Ann imagined him in the years before, dusting the spare furniture, poking at spider webs under chairs, eating his cold cereal in the parlor. It had been his club; he took his vacations there. Now none of them treated downstairs as home. We live here, she thought, as if it were a rooming house. We are only comfortable when asleep. We do not dare get up for a glass of water at night. Some nights I will forget or not care and go down the stairs without putting on the lights and I will bump into David standing in the dark or I will touch him by mistake or because I want to and I will forget that he is sixty-eight and my father-in-law.

Last week when she had gone to the rose garden because he had asked so many times and the frost might come any night, he had taken her hand when he was helping her over the soft white earth heaped up around the bushes. "You stand there, between those two beauties, and I'll take your picture for Phil." She had bent to smell the petals big as tongues, but there was no scent. "They're too perfect to smell. They're bred for looks. Smile for Phil now."

She worried about whether her face in the photograph would show her fear and surprise. Of course, he had to help me over the ground; I might have lost my balance in heels and fallen on the roses, and he's an old-fashioned man. Theresa had expected him to open doors and raise his hat. Naturally, he would reach out to help any woman, especially if he invited her to the park, which is really like his kingdom. He often kissed Francie when she had made a special effort to dress up for Jim on a Saturday night, and he gave Phil a bear hug at the start and end of his Wednesday visits to the hospital. His hand, Ann remembered from the rose garden, had been soft and warm. She had expected it to be rough and perhaps cold. In general he had grown old in the un- noticeable way animals do, gradually gaining white hairs, and his eyes shone from nests of small wrinkles. He did not walk like an old man, and he did not twitch or pace. Watching the slow growth of lovely silent things, he was submerged in pa- tience.

How ridiculous I am, Ann thought, my kind father-in-law helps me into the rose garden, and I dwell on his courtesy until I turn it into sin. I must put a decent future together. I must find a hospital nearer that will take Phil so that I can visit him every evening. We should never have come here to live. I should have tried to manage in Akron somehow. Be- fore Francie marries, I must find an apartment for myself near Phil's hospital. Otherwise, Dave and I will forget who we are, and we could go strange.

Years ago when Ann was in grammar school, one of her best friends, Doris Wobluda, who wore a red coat with a little raccoon collar, was taken by a lady who had come in a state car from the classroom and questioned in the vestibule where they kept their coats and lunch boxes. Doris came back crying, and the woman told her to bring along her pencil case and everything that belonged to her in the desk. They drove away in the state car. After school Ann told her mother, who nodded. They had taken Doris away to live somewhere else. Her father was a bad man and he had done something against the law. No one would tell what it was. Sliding downhill into a stalky field beside the school, she asked all her friends what they thought Doris Wobluda's father had done. One thought it might have something to do with sucking blood; another had heard the word, mistreatment. For a second the door of the slaughter house and the window of the savages' temple swung open. Most of them were easily frightened children: pictures of the Visigoths in the history book and photographs of boa constrictors made them cry. They crossed the street before coming to the Wobludas' old house, but the name was scratched from the mailbox and a clump of For Sale signs stood in the weedy lawn.

She thought of the Wobludas again when Francie was in junior high in Akron, and a neighbor who had never spoken to her appeared at the screen door one August afternoon and asked to have a word with Ann. "I feel it my duty to tell you what queer people have moved in near the traffic light. They run that paper store, and you wouldn't want Francie to go there."

"Why? What could happen," Ann asked.

"Oh, it's not what could, but what has. Have you had a good look at them?"

"Why?"

"You'll see what I mean. There's that old man, that awful old man, with the weak chin, and his wife—you never see her. But there's the daughter, the nervous one that laughs. You've seen her dumping garbage and such. Look at those children of hers. It's terrible. They have the map of her father's face pasted on theirs."

"Lots of us look like our grandparents."

"There are ways." The visitor shook her head. "It's their influence on our own, I worry about. We can't be safe with them at the corner. You have to know about such things these days."

Ann put off visiting the store, but one day with lowered eyes grimly searched for a birthday card, slid the quarter along the counter toward the grandfather, refused a bag, and in a rush to leave the store dropped the card on the floor. "Here. I'll get you a fresh one," the grandfather said, picking up the stained envelope at her feet. Had he touched her shoulder when he passed the new card to her? He opened the door and said: "Watch your step now." She looked fiercely at him, as she walked out, amazed by his gentle smile. She was surprised that murderers standing trial were neatly dressed and often handsome. The grandfather melted into a nighttime gallery of exiles—the insurance salesman who liked to embroider samplers when the shades were pulled down, the grown man who still slept in his parents' bedroom, the brother and sister who drove through the dark lanes of the forest preserve sitting close together in the front seat of the Dodge. How do we know these details of strangers' lives, she wonered; do they want us to know? Maybe it's not strangeness any more but part of themselves, and they no longer care about what we do or think.

A few years ago she could have put herself to sleep by remembering the shape of Phil's mouth as it had been, but lately her hot brain could not focus past midnight on any face, old or new. There is so much more to life than love, she thought, twisting on the mattress, so much more than twenty or thirty minutes a week and never as good as you plotted it to be, sometimes only a bad headache, sore muscles, and a great thirst. But without its possibility, you stand like a summer trellis in a frost-bitten garden.

The wind shivered the pennants around the Esso station and rocked the leaf shadows on her ceiling. Jim's car rustled to the curb, and Francie strode quickly through the small house to her room. Always a separate child, she had not inspired passion. She had not liked to be picked up or squeezed, but suffered caresses as a cat might. She was thoughtful of both parents and patient with Phil's sickness. It would be a simple matter to lose Francie to marriage because she had not really been there at all.

Like a hawk perfectly poised to be lifted by a wind current, Ann waited for sleep. Her tense heels and her outstretched palms pressed her up from the bed into a dream.

THE SAVED

MAN

❧ The sheets fell away from Dr. Roger Longo. Through the Venetian blinds he was all planes and shafts falling. Everything fell away. He grunted, coughed, the dry gargle of a forty-year-old, overweight, summer-neglected husband. He pulled himself up on one elbow. Outside, steel heels beat furiously on the sidewalk, angry with Sunday. They will push us into it, bury us with their steel heels, he thought, and got up to prevent its happening today.

For two weeks Marion and the children had telephoned from half across the country great news of prairie dogs and rodeos. They were spending the month with Marion's parents driving toward the Golden Gate, stopping at every reptile museum, reading every historical marker, and trying to figure out what the nation was about.

He slid his feet into loafers and scuffed toward the kitchen to load the perculator, the sugar bowl, creamer, toaster, cat's bowl, then the garbage—enough to keep Quong Hue, crippled Vietnamese five-year-old, sole support of depressed parents and three siblings, in good cheer for a week, all from the morning's breakfast. That consideration destroyed the coffee and weakened the juice. He went on murdering his own pleasures as they were born. The things a man might do alone that he saves for all through the winter and the spring, where were they now? He had bought all the raw materials against this time: water colors, German camera with reflexes faster than his own—to master them; perhaps to improve his handwriting into an italic hand or learn Japanese paper folding or to read the Psalms. Nothing had come of them and he would put off failure a little by getting to St. Sebastian's for the eleven o'clock Alka-Seltzer Mass.

·　　　·　　　·

Flo slept deadly but holding fast lest she slip, by forgetting one breath. Her hands and feet were clenched; even her teeth ground against each other; her chin was locked to her breast, her blind mind swam through gray-green hoops, barnacle crusted, flippers waving past black windows of sunken ship-houses, heavy divers' hands pawed at delicate locks, struggled to raise silent things—amphora, death masks, weighted all in sea water. Limp eels, sparking dimly, slithered past her thighs. Strings of air bubbles gargled upward and away. She dreamed and swam, and warm arteries pulsed. She arched toward the surface to touch the land again, opened her fingers, spread her toes and was—somewhat—awake.

The ship that was her bed was old, warped, shoved like an afterthought into a dusty alcove. It was in a basement, under the underpinnings of the house, the intertwined and shrouded pipes creaking and groaning above her head. Now, of course, they were silently and emptily waiting. The cheap simple-faced alarm said five-fifteen. As always, she had beaten the alarm; perhaps it had gotten tired of trying to surprise her and had lost its voice a long time ago.

She was wearing a thin pair of men's pajamas—the waist elastic worn out—tied with a piece of clothes line in the middle. One thing she hardly ever wore in the summer here was shoes, except in rain. Her toes no longer felt the sand between them. She stretched, one young, jerky stretch, and walked to a wire hanger over a window and took off a faded red tank suit.

When she took off clothes, she shucked down to the flesh and left the old ones in a pile or kicked them under something, the bed, chairs, whatever was closest.

The red tank suit gripped, elastic all over. She rubbed her belly, tried to pull the suit down over her thighs, found a rubber cap, and sealed her head into it.

The beach was thirty feet from the door—so close the cellar flooded every fall and spring and smelled always of salt and mold.

The water was sudden, gray, and sharp. She crouched and splashed, then slid into it and became, yes, became seaborne. Surf and waves met, bucked. She slid through, pushed, plunged, pushed, and cut through. Free now, her mind was for a while lead, stopped, then beyond the waves crinkled into thought. One memory trumpeted to the center.

In the '48 Olympics in London, an Australian—the one in the 200-meter breast stroke—was asking her why she liked free-style at all. They had been sitting, swinging legs over the edge during the prelims, watching scrubbers clean out and fill the great pool. He was a big man and wore a red beard too. All wrong looking for the 200 meter—who are always compact, little-headed men, but he sat, Reggie Baylis, he was, waving his arms, not saving an ounce, and slapping the tiles with his palms, a wonderful figure of a man, lovely arm muscles. In the water his feet moved to music. Never saw a dancer like him.

She was gap-toothed and hated to show it, but smiled largely at Reggie Baylis, who didn't notice. Reggie looked a little beyond them. She was always good at the warm-up and first laps, not so good with the home stretch. For a while after he went back to Perth they sent letters, but swimmers aren't good writers, so it was Christmas cards and then Reggie Baylis faded from the green pool, probably declined into sporting goods.

The sun spilled straight out to the shore, burning off the tails of haze. She paddled like a seal, turned over to bob a while on her back—about two miles out now. From north, Marblehead, kapluck, kapluck, kapluck, the coast guard cutter on its six-thirty run was gray on gray. They met misty morning May to September. She rolled her arms like busy windmills, showing off.

From the bow, an earnest, apple-cheeked sailor: "Hi, Flo. On time? How's it feel this morning? Freeze your rear off?"

"Come down and see," she, floating, holding the bottom rung of the ladder. "I'd give you a free lesson. Never lost a pupil yet."

"I'm allergic to water. No kidding. I hate the stuff. There must be some easier way to earn a living than this."

The boat idled. When the engines churned dryly fast again, she took off toward the shore and a slow run through the Sunday papers.

. . .

Roger's was not an old missal; it simply looked old. They get shabby fast. About a thousand pages of extra-thin onion skin, always sticking together, calendar through 1977 or the end of the world. Today, September second, the thirteenth Sunday after Pentecost, was St. Stephen's day, not the Martyr, but the King Confessor, the Hungarian, for whom the big dark cathedral in Vienna was named. In the basement, beneath the high altar the weaseled Austrian with steel teeth, who was showing Roger through, stopped at a round something like a well and beckoned him to its edge. He peered into a circle of pure black. "They throw bones," the Austrian insisted. Whose bones? Why? When? Divided by language, they stood at the stone rim, smelling down into dust of bone before climbing to the square and pasteries on the Johannesgasse.

So what other mark had Stephen made? He read the collect: Grant we may practice with befitting zeal the faith of thy blessed confessor, Stephen. That was all for Stephen: dusty bones and one line of zeal.

Roger was a fast and nervous reader. He grazed through the back of the missal—prayers for special occasions, churching women after childbirth, prayer for the king and his family chanted in some countries after last Mass on Sunday, prayer in time of famine and pestilence, collects for the martyrs like John de Breheuf and Isaac Joques with the destroyed hands.

He was always being yanked back and never reading in the right place, the Epistle during the Gospel, the Credo too rapidly, never got on the same time schedule as any priest, except for the fifteen-minute navy ones. When he had been in the daily Mass habit, it went fast, his timing faultless. At the Cross, he went every day, everybody did, no virtue in that. The prefect knocked at quarter to six; you slid from communion to breakfast to a smoke and then chemistry or whatever. At Georgetown he began missing, no excuse, a chapel on the first floor of the hospital, but after handling flesh and changing dressings nothing can wash your hands properly. At first, he smelled them all the time.

So now, now, he was Sunday-lost in giant daily missal and even cheating his way into the English column where once he had read straight through the Latin. The thirteenth Sunday after Pentecost—the ten lepers crying from afar, made clean, from whom alone the Samaritan threw his face into the dust in gratitude, "*Surge vade*; your faith has made you whole." Where did the nine go? Why only this unexpected foreigner in gratitude? Roger saw this Samaritan scraping off the old white skin for new pink underneath, enjoying his spot in the dust, sloppily proclaiming his eternal debt: "Doc, I'll never forget you, never. As long as I draw a breath, Doc, I'll remember I owe my life to you. Ask me for anything, Doc, anything. You can have it. Name my next kid for you. Anything, Doc."

Just pay the bill. Stop drooling.

The nine ungrateful and the one worthy were all hustled dustily away. The last summer Sunday had no sermon, no rambling exhortation for the dearly beloved toward evening devotion, to read and ponder the *Pilot* every Thursday, to recreate the Holy Family in deepest Mattapan, to frequent the sacraments, to be scraped clean along with the spotty Samaritan.

Spud Cullinan scooted down the aisle to beat the Sanctus, genuflected vigorously, reached behind the vigil lights to find the basket. He was advancing too rapidly on Roger, who was digging into his wallet, undecided about a one or a fiver. He finally threw his lot with two ones and folded them into the smallest possible square, just as Spud bent over his shoulder in a cloud of King's Men after-shave: "How you doing, buddy boy?" Obviously, this was going to be a double operation, the monthly collection too. The second wave of collectors came, spatter, pong, cling, up the aisle on Spud's trail.

The child in front of him dropped her dime and crawled under the pew, finding it beneath Roger's kneeler. Her mother jerked her upward by one shoulder and swatted her in a flash. She rocketed into one scream, cascaded down in gushing sobs. All around the church, children joined the chorus. Up on the altar, the microphone caught the priest's asthmatic breathing before the Consecration. He had, Roger remembered, complained of shortness of breath, and his heart was unusually enlarged, even for sixty-five. Probably keel over one cold morning in the sacristy—no difficulty imagining him a corpse, halfway there now. Lots of people have coronaries in church. Well, a lot of people do in buses or stores. Waiting for something to happen isn't good for some people.

Roger stared at the Cana window, gift of the Curran family.

A stern Jesus, high eyebrows, pert beard, red cloak, instructed
the round-faced workmen in short togas in the jug business.
Mary, in blue, had asserted control and stood nonchalantly
beside the open door through which the happy couple and
guests would be. And where was Joseph? Where was Joseph
ever?

Tears had worn out the child in front. She leaned, mouth
open and drooling, against her mother. Everyone waited, lost
and spent, and nothing happened. They were frozen, each in
a private block. The ushers had counted the collections and
stood, legs apart, with their hands behind their backs. An
altar boy scratched his nose. They were all suspended until
the moment of release after the priest's blessing.

The parking lot became a madhouse. Cars roared across
the white lines and jammed the narrow exits. A wide station
wagon darkly filled with children throbbed by Roger's ankles
with six inches to spare.

It was noon when he drove into another parking lot at the
hospital: he had only one patient here to see, and she was
certainly not making a ceremony of dinner. The hospital was
modern enough to hide its function. It might almost have
been any kind of office building, that is, if you had never been
in a hospital. The floors and walls in various sections were in
ambiguous colors chosen not to antagonize or inspire or even
please. Great baskets of flowers freshly sent from funeral
homes leaned against the corridors.

"Hi there, Dr. Longo, how're you doing?" the charge nurse
asked, showing all her teeth.

"Fine. How's yourself?" He always wanted to shock her

with a careless obscenity, but at the last moment always lost his nerve.

Into first-floor semi-private. If he looked closely, a little hump sank against the bars as if someone had shaken all the feathers of a not-very-large pillow into the bottom and had pushed it almost out of the bed.

"And how is Mrs. Schenkel?" Does Mrs. Schenkel know herself? Living or dead? Hard to tell. Pressure nonexistent. If alive, so by the grace of cortisone, anticoagulant, dextrose, teriomycin. Brain damage, ninety per cent. Incapable of speech or motor activity, refusing death by common pneumonia, embolism, hemorrhage, awaiting something more exotic. Her privilege, he told himself again.

What Mrs. Schenkel had looked like in civilian life was impossible to guess. She might have been born a few years ago in Room 119. Listening to her squeaky lungs, he decided he would leave immediately for the beach. Mrs. Schenkel's best office in the last eighteen months had been to inspire complete and pure selfishness in anyone coming into Room 119. That is why Roger went to great lengths to put the top down, to go home for more money, more food.

The beach, when he got there, was the usual modern zoo, arranged in family clusters. From cubicles at the headlands came shrieks and thumps; below, the equipment spread, covering all the sand—aluminum cots, barbecue grills, blazing flesh, blazing charcoal, gritty hands stroking oil into gritty backs, hairy thighs and glossy ribs and breasts, bodies bound in some spots, released to bulge against straps and cuffs.

A woman in a faded red tank suit was standing in the cen-

ter of a mob of children. They were all suspended, patches of
color and elbows and heels, saving their dash for—was it a
whistle or a distant mother's voice? Roger recognized their
keeper, not by name but type. Women like that taught dancing on Saturday mornings in the winter in the ballrooms of
hotels. And a one and two and three; one-two-three, thump-
thump-thump. Ramrod accompanist striking the piano like
a drum. Learn box step, and life and love and opportunity
open for you for evermore. They yawn for you. The women
who gave the box step in the winter gave the Australian
crawl and the breast stroke in July, baton twirling and bowling stands in between. They were like old ballerinas, flat-
chested, splendid thighs—one long obedient muscle from
head to toe. They had shown their bodies so long and carelessly and pedagogically that they forfeited being female.
They were old children.

This one blew her whistle and, as he knew they would, the
children poured their energy into some elaborate design,
right hand on next left shoulder, and began to march toward
the water. But at the edge they spun and twirled and were
separate again and screamed at different pitches. The woman
stood waist-deep, a Gulliver, exhorting them to keep their
heads low and to push, p-u-s-h with their feet, that's right,
now push— Their silky flesh rolled past her sharp hips, slid
through the little waves with inbuilt vigor. Thin necks, tiny
bones—that's what pediatricians felt all day, rib cages the
size of turkeys', with frantic hearts rattling inside.

He walked back to lie on a sand mound and shut his eyes
against the silver heat.

A lump bothered his elbow. He scratched at the sand. He was always pulling and rubbing and feeling: as a kid twirling loose teeth or running his fingers fast around the embossed anchors on the buttons of his sailor coat or grabbing for the pussy willows as he went by. Marion was always telling him to quit picking at his face. He would stop an instant and then be back on the old ridges and valleys. At night his feet met and rubbed against each other, and in the morning his face wore strange little scratches. Now those futile steel-springed paws were working away in the sand, uncovering half of a big ugly shell, gull-abandoned. And this stupid white platter had once been its bones. They wear their bones on the outside, and this one—large, flat, and somewhat yellow-stained on the inside, was Roger Longo, exactly what he would have looked like reincarnated as a mollusk. That was real, but damned depressing.

He decided to try the water and walked down the beach into the brilliant flock of young swimmers. This, September second, was the first time in the whole summer that he'd gone in. All his nerves stood up together and strained skin-ward when the icy water hit his belly, but he sprang fast and let himself be carried over a giant roller. He was strong and fast at first but tired easily. He passed all the landbound and pretending swimmers and was pushing himself all alone through the little white peaks when a ganglia of pain exploded into the corners of his body, which were hundreds of miles from his heart. I am drowning, he thought. This is the way I will die. I have lived what seems a long time, but I can not think of anything I want to remember now. He was surprised at not being more sorry or afraid—as he sank and his shut eyes saw only a bed of purple coals.

·   ·   ·

She rapped the stiff white petals of a flowered bathing cap in front of her. "Keep your head down, down, and your elbows in-in-in." A vacant-faced boy was looking toward the lighthouse on the point.

"Don't be lazy, Edgar. Get down again."

"There was a man out there, Flo. Not there any more. He's gone."

"So? That isn't any of your business. Down, Edgar."

"But, he's gone under, Flo." His face was strained with intensity, perhaps truth.

She dove, a tight half-circle. A couple of hundred feet out she found a wave trying to decide what to do with Roger Longo, who was beyond caring himself. Her left arm wrapped round his shoulders, she kicked slowly back toward shore, while the children stood silent in their shallow world.

He lay, staining the sand. She felt the bones of his face soft under the wet skin, when she put her lips over his. He was a long time coming around. His throat and sinuses gave up rivulets of brine. She sucked so deep that where her breath ended and his began it was hard to tell. Then his eyelids flickered and strained to stay half open.

The enormity of thanking her sat heavily on his mind. His mouth was salt-washed, bubbles rose in his chest, but he repeated the truth carefully: "I nearly drowned out there, and you saved me. I'm supposed to make people live, but you saved me."

She was unimpressed by his statement or the situation and was shooing the children homeward, although they all wanted to stay and see the freshly drowned man rise and walk to Flo's basement. Inside it was dark, warm, and thinly furnished. He sank into a brittle wicker chair which squeaked. Flo began making tea and pulling china out of a cabinet. From a corner of the floor she took a chenille bathrobe, which she put on before she brought the tea and sat on an equally squeaky chair opposite his.

"I've always wondered," she began.

"About what?"

"Your kind—doctors. Like in another country. Whether they give up looking at people."

"How could we? No, when we're working, we only see pieces of bodies, never whole, and the landscape's never a very pretty one: old scars and the whole genealogy of pain, mistakes perpetuated over and over again, staining every damn tissue."

"But there *are* perfect ones."

"Only in the anatomy books."

"In high school, I used to look at the plates in the back of the dictionary," she said.

"So did we all. How do you think we ever began at first? Nothing is the way it is in books. Like the heart. It's always somewhere you're not looking for it—fatty tissue on top, or almost under the sternum."

"And not pretty?"

"What?"

"The heart. I mean, it's not like on valentines." She spoke English carefully, a little as if it were a foreign language, or perhaps words, even small ones, were too large for her mouth. Then he decided she just didn't talk much. She was out of practice.

"No, not at all like a valentine, more like a great fist. It gets larger as you grow older."

"That's odd. It seemed to me it would shrink, but then it has more to worry about." She saw a great house frantically adding red chambers to accommodate the spreading.

"No, not like that. It's harder to pump. There's more of us for the blood to get around." He patted his own paunch. They were both embarrassed. A cicada high in the elm outside sawed and stopped short. The sun stretched across the gray sandy floor.

"Have you ever noticed how all still places have their own kinds of silence?" Her voice died into its own silence.

"You live here all year?" he asked.

"No, I'm a beach bum. Fort Lauderdale in the winter. I rent the upstairs to a camel. You know, one of those men who runs a junk shop on the boardwalk—Persian rugs and Meissen statues, all made in Tokyo—going out of business, sacrifice prices, everything must go, from May to September."

"You always lived here?"

"Heavens, no. I grew up in Nebraska beside a river that was dry in the summer after tiring itself out flooding in the spring."

He noticed a bronze ashtray filled with candy wrappers. In the middle of it was a green mermaid, which she saw him staring at. "Just think, I posed for the top of that. My family about killed me when they found out, but you figure as you

grow older the body you had before isn't yours any more, so
it doesn't matter. Isn't that right?"

"Well, in a way we are always what we started out to be,"
he said, lamely.

Another cicada climbed dizzily until it choked.

"My father," she said, "poor man, he was mad."

"Oh," he asked, "how?"

"He suffered from uselessness."

"It's the worst disease, but we all do some of the time."

"It ate him particularly, like a corn borer."

"Why especially him?"

She poured more tea. "This pot put me in mind of him.
He made it. He was from Stokes originally, and he came to
the States fired up to make dinner sets for the masses. You
know how he wound up? Toilet fixtures. And the dreams that
man had. He *would* make Nanking jars and spatterware plates
and Gaudy Dutch sugarbowls, but nobody wanted them. He
worked late at night and Sundays in a shed behind the house.
He made a kiln and in those cold nights he fired it, so you
could see the red eyes of the fire through one window of the
shed. He made sets and sets of dishes."

"Who used them?"

"We had to. Every week he broke the ones we'd been using
and started over again. He talked to himself when he was
working and shouted and screamed and at last they had to
ask him to commit himself."

Roger looked at the teapot. It was brown glaze, a little
lopsided, it seemed. Something should be said.

"Insane is just a word."

"I'm sorry. I oughtn't to have brought him up. That was ancient history. It's like a couple of oceans away."

It was late afternoon. He wanted to leave and to stay and, most of all, to pay. How do I pay, he wondered. They teach you so many things and always the wrong ones. There had never been anything about how you could pay someone for saving your life.

"I have to go home now." She looked at his lying lips, not countering with any invitation. "I'd like to tell you how much . . . What I mean is, I'm alive."

"So you are," she said, smiling. "Yes, you'd better go."

He reached across the table and took her hand, which was firm and cool. "Thank you. I'm leaving the swimming to the professionals."

He kept thinking of what he should have said for months, deep into the next winter.

SUNDAY'S
CHILDREN

◆§◈ At three-fifteen on the last Sunday afternoon of October Virginia Scanlan parked her car outside a funhouse on the boardwalk at Point of Firs. The funhouse, officially the Jungle of Horrors, was boarded up—had been boarded up for ten years. Ginny put down the sun visor and began reading an old issue of the *Digest* she kept in the glove compartment and had been reading off and on for several months. Before she got through two paragraphs of the condensed novel, all three hands of her watch crossed each other at 3:19. That might be a sign, but she couldn't act on only one of them. She looked around for another test. If the old gull squatting on the boardwalk flew toward her, she would start the car and drive past Steve Cleary's house. If the gull flew toward the beach, she would go back home and wash some blouses. It took the gull a long time to decide to move and then it only hopped around in a big circle cocking its head. Finally it half ran toward Ginny's car and looked affronted as she started the car and ground the gears.

When she reached Steve's street, she considered the possible tactics. She could crawl along at the lowest possible speed, not turning her head, but shifting her eyes toward the porch where he might be sitting. Or she could speed along as if her life depended on getting off that street and then with great surprise at seeing him, jam on the brakes and back to his front walk.

She arranged her face for the indifferent rush, but a hundred tics wrecked her mask. And naturally her plan to roar the length of the street crumbled. At that moment she hoped he wouldn't be there at all, and then she could go home to the unwashed blouses and the long nap. But it was too late for that; Steve Cleary was taken, surprised, raking leaves in his front yard. Although she had been plotting this moment all day, she saw him as a stranger, guarding his lawn with a bamboo rake. His mother made him wear glasses at home. The weight of them seemed to make the rest of his face sag down to his big chin.

"Well, hello." He could not pretend to be happy at seeing Ginny.

The open smile she'd practiced on the street fell away, and she gave her face over entirely to the tics. She concentrated all her energy on getting an offhand tone into her voice, but all that came out was a squeak. "Could you come out with me for a little while now?"

He dug the bamboo rake into the grass. "I'd like to. I would. But my mother has this leaf project lined up. She wants them burned."

"Oh. Well it doesn't matter. I just thought it was a nice day, and I happened to be driving by. That's all."

Somewhere Mrs. Cleary listened behind the screen door, from the garage, from the back porch. She would be standing, her shaking head stretched ahead of her body on a rigid neck. She could not give Ginny Scanlan the satisfaction of seeing her raking leaves. Mrs. Cleary sharpened her dislike for Ginny at breakfast every morning and by afternoon it was very well polished.

"Perhaps later. I'll get done in an hour or so and then we can go to a movie or something. Could you meet me down-street at five?"

His voice at home was a little above a whisper. It was as if he was giving her a lesson in lip reading, to which she was sup-posed to respond with the right sign. She nodded and drove away from the enemy castle before the wicked witch came out on her rake.

She was no Gretel, by a damned sight, not at thirty-five. And he was no Hansel either, not at forty on his last birth-day. Nor did Mrs. Cleary make a very good witch. Her sin and sorrow lay in living too long, which she knew well but denied hourly by making great promises of what she would do next week, next year, when she got on her feet again and settled a few things, when the buyer arrived for the house, when she moved into a little place of her own. In her seventy-fifth year she talked of a fresh start and so she kept surprising the day by getting up earlier and earlier, scratching in the pantry and kitchen in the thin hours before dawn, eating a second breakfast on the stove fender a few hours later when Steve came downstairs at six.

Each morning he searched for signs of new decay with

horror and satisfaction, which might be told in the dropping of a dish or fit of tears. But every year she reckoned on more weakness and shrewdly studied ways to lean her chin on her hand to hide the shaking, to conceal the liver spots on her hands by wearing gloves, to change the subject when she forgot names. Steve patched the weak spots in the dike, bought new glasses with built-in hearing aids and space shoes and tranquilizers before Mame Cleary knew they made such things and before she'd studied how to avoid them. Most of the time when Steve was around she sat hidden behind the stove, often in the dark to save the electricity, and waited for the plain clock with Roman numbers to tell the half hours or the hours. Then she listened to five minutes of the news. When he was not there, she probably sneaked around the house the way women do, but still listened to the news or worried about whether the clock was right. She was cheerful, except on the subject of Virginia Scanlan, and if you asked how she felt, she always said: "A hundred per cent."

About old age Ginny knew a few things too. She had buried two grandmothers, one miserable and fat who got eaten with cancer, the other gentle and thin who died the night of Ginny's high school graduation. After the grandmothers came great-aunts and great-uncles who didn't count because they sickened and decayed elsewhere. The present source of information was her own mother who spent the nights crying out names and imperative sentences from behind the door of the bedroom she no longer shared with Mr. Scanlan, who could not climb stairs after his last stroke. It took him a long time to scuff from the living room sofa that was his bed to the kitchen table, but once there he ate like a horse and he listened to all the Red Sox games and he always knew who Ginny was. It could have been much worse.

She drove back to the funhouse, parked again, and tried to read the condensed novel. But she found herself reading the wrong words. This kept happening. On the table of contents "Snore Cures" became "Snake Crews." Something called "Are We Picking the Right President?" was "Are We Picking the Night Residue?" Too tired, she supposed. Even the newspapers were too hard. She would really have liked to go back home and sleep away the afternoon. But her suburb was almost on the other side of the city, and now that she'd made this much of a fool of herself, she deserved to sit there.

The town Steve had always lived in was on the shore. Once the city had pushed itself that far, it gave up and left behind its pretenses: strings of bungalows with scrawny gardens behind them. But the city had never been able to convert Point of Firs to urban ways. One defense against that was the amusement park, never really successful. Even in its best years it had been shabby. Then as fires and bankruptcies made bigger gaps along the boardwalk, the season became shorter and the rides fewer. The roller coaster finally sagged and stopped running. The Democrats and the PTA held state conventions in the great Typee Ballroom with the revolving stained-glass chandelier. They did not use the chandelier, of course, but Steve remembered Saturday night dances in the 1930's—when girls with long black hair swung their accordion-pleated skirts toward and away from thin sailor suits of the coastguardsmen from the lighthouse station.

And over them flickered little spectrum rainbows as the chandelier turned and the Hawaiian guitar rippled. Steve had stood, sucking softly, on the straws of his coke on the edge of the floor, concentrating on these pleasures of the future before wheeling home.

The last dance in the Grand Typee Ballroom, which was really moderate sized and without a single similarity to a wigwam, had been in the summer of '47. Steve, freshly out of the Air Force, had taken a young war widow from the South who was waiting to find out what to do next. He couldn't remember her face now, but she had had a very good time at the dance and, wanting to repay him, she stroked his neck and shoulders fiercely as he drove her home to her apartment. He never became a very good driver and that night was a clumsy memory. After the summer the war widow found out what to do and moved away from the sea where her husband's body had disappeared. With her went her little girl—Steve had liked the kid—and they never had another dance in the Grand Typee Ballroom.

"It's the kind of town," he often said to Ginny, "you wish you didn't live in, so you could visit it. When you're born into it, where's there to go?"

She nodded. What else could you say? And in five years of almost every Wednesday and some Sundays, they'd improvised on what they had to say until the topics were threadbare and no new skein of talk could lighten the pattern or patch the holes. Perhaps they had not talked that much and they had only had so much chance to think before and during conversations and so much time to review them afterward that a dialogue went on in their heads day after day. She knew the name of Steve's third-grade teacher—Elaine Grassi Igoe—and about the Christmas his father had gotten five watches at one time and wore all of them, and the grand doings of his service buddy Fish Dunlop, who still drank a fifth of Old Crow every day and a half, and the way his grandfather, a union organizer, had looked when the heart attack grabbed him—about to push a company truck loaded with cotton bales into the Merrimack in February of 1934. He had all her stories, her relatives, her failures in his head, and except that the silences were too hard to take, they would have walked speechless through their Wednesday and Sunday nights.

"What do you talk about with Tim?" she asked her sister one night over the dishes. But her sister, long married, had looked up from scrubbing the broiler and waited for her to smile as if it were a joke. No answer. After that she took to listening for a few weeks to the conversations of her married friends. Not all of them talked all the time, but what they said was about their children and their children's sicknesses or teachers or cars and vacations. They seldom mentioned their youth, which was mostly what she talked about with Steve. Ginny supposed that marriage gave them new topics—enough to last ten years or so—and new things to do when the conversation wouldn't run.

Wednesday nights had no silences. At five o'clock she went into the relief room and put on new lipstick and her suede pumps and then stood waiting in the parking lot. This avoided his going all through the reception line in her living room.

Her father thwacking his evening *Traveler* with his one good hand and croaking: "You look like a damned Christmas tree on stilts." Her mother's "Have a nice time, dear," as if they were all caught up in an Andy Hardy movie or maybe one of those comic strips where for twenty years nobody gets a day older.

Anyway, the living room, more than the rest of the house, was an old battlefield, and it could never mean the same thing to a sightseer, even the veteran of an almost identical campaign. So they met in the neutral ground of the company parking lot and drove back slowly to the Best Value store in Beale Square, where they got out. Anybody seeing them would have thought they were late shoppers, getting a bottle of milk for morning coffee. For Steve, who had managed the Beale Square supermarket for six years, closing time was very much like church.

He stood beside the door unlocking it as each stacker and checker took off his apron, hung it on a hook in the back closet, and shrugged himself into the unfamiliar coat. "'Night, Joe, Ed, Frank, Bud. 'Night, Mr. Cote." Steve would never be on first-name basis with the butcher, Mr. Cote, a long-faced aristocrat. Most butchers are prima donnas, and good ones like Cote deserved respect. The door was automatic, but Steve held it open anyway for Cote, who, like a captain, waited for everyone else to leave.

Behind, the music now silent, Ginny walked up and down between towers of cans under the faint whine of neon lights. The raw materials of eating mystified her, the choices of size and substance and color, the casual tone of cookbooks, no comfort in a frenzied kitchen. She had never fixed a whole meal in her life; the kitchen was her mother's as clearly as if the range were padlocked against intruders. Any interest in cooking Ginny might ever have owned had withered and died. Once in the summer at a beach picnic for the store she sat watching Steve confidently season and broil a mound of steaks. She had been frozen by the fear someone would ask her to toss a salad and she would drop the lettuce on the sand. But no one asked her to do anything, and their not asking made her sick. She was often sick. "You get your bad stomach from your father," her mother said. The only kind of food she liked was what you got at drug store counters.

Steve drove the scattered pushcarts into each other. He was pleased with their two neat rows, not so happy about the clumps of unsold bread and the fat African violets that refused to bloom and sell themselves. Until the last he saved the rolls of sales slips from the cash registers. He lifted them carefully off the machines and locked them into the safe in the glassed-in square he called his office to look at first thing in the morning. Then he remembered Ginny and found her staring into a bin of frozen turkey pies.

"Have you ever had one?" she asked.

"Never." He was shocked she thought his mother capable of that.

"How can they be sure that twenty-five minutes at three hundred and fifty degrees does the trick?"

"It's all worked out. Somebody in a big kitchen in St. Paul or Grand Rapids decides all the frozen turkey pies in America need twenty-five minutes. Like the cake mixes."

There were a good many Wednesday nights when she would rather have gone right home from work and he would rather have stayed in the store adding up the sales slips, but they always went to the Miter for drinks and dinner. They had three martinis and listened to Honey Holman, a nice girl with a long neck, play "When the Red, Red Robin Comes Bob, Bob, Bobbing Along" on the Hammond organ. The Miter served hot hors d'oeuvres which tasted exactly like the dinner so it was hard to know when the dinner began or ended. They knew everybody at the Miter—the waitresses, Sam Rosten who owned it, Honey Holman, and a lot of the salesmen who stayed in the hotel above. Steve usually invited some of them to have a cordial at his table after dinner, so there was plenty of talk there and enough afterward in the car going home.

The rest of the week after work she went bowling and took her nieces and nephews to get new shoes or wrote letters or found relatives for her mother to visit. He played the drums in a very good marching band that rehearsed twice a week and made a number of appearances on weekends. One of the big network shows had them on TV, and *Life* had done a piece on them.

On Sundays usually they went to the movies and had dinner at the Four Elms, skipping the drinks. Without mentioning where they were going, but with everybody knowing, they edged out of their houses on discreet excuses about meeting friends, ransoming the evening with elaborate promises of being back soon, which they would be. Sundays were never as good as Wednesdays. On the crest of the week of work, they rolled through Wednesdays. On Sundays they met like strangers, kept their masks glued on, and left gratefully when the time was up. Sometimes when there were band concerts or leaves to be raked, they skipped the Sundays entirely. On a couple of those nights one of them might drive across the city and peak through the window at the other, sitting in the living room in front of the TV set, and then return home.

So this October Sunday she had thrown a wrench into the schedule by coming in the middle of the leaf-raking. But the cost of driving up to his house seemed to her to offset her intrusion.

When he got out of his car, she saw that he had changed. At a certain age, people stop wearing their clothes and let the clothes take over. Ginny knew his suits all hung in his closet with his shape still in them as the arms of her dresses rested against the stiff arms of others.

They walked along the boardwalk, she on tiptoe to keep her heels from being caught in the holes; he thought women wore heels on Sunday. She was careful to hold her arm rigid so that the charm bracelet wouldn't rattle. They had given each other every gift they could think of and he had settled on the bracelet to which he kept adding charms. It was a very heavy bracelet. It had a motorcycle with movable wheels, a telephone with moving dial, a tennis racket, a Christmas tree, a replica of the Miss America statue, and one of most of the animals in the Ark.

The movie theater had been built at the same time as the Grand Typee Ballroom. Its ceiling wore irregular rows of bulbs, between other rows of thick-necked cherubs. On both side walls paintings of tall austere women who might have been Indian or Greek raised orange torches.

"This is supposed to be good," Steve said. "It got four stars. The *Post* had an article about it. They filmed it in Spain, but it really happened in Nebraska."

"Who goes to find out how many stars to give it?" She was looking around the shattered and scuffed seats before the lights went out. They were the two oldest people there. Everybody else was the child of somebody Steve had gone to high school with. Ginny watched them attempting to knot their supple arms around each other and noticed how they lost hold and slipped away and then wrestled back, trying to find a comfortable embrace. The lights went out.

The movie was about two couples who spent a great deal of time in the kitchen of one set. The two couples were learning that they had married the wrong people. One husband and the other wife could have managed very well, but the second wife, miserable with her husband's silence and their bills and his drinking, went crying into the night and was blinded by a speeding car and killed in the rain. Her husband, guilty and unshaven, sat with the other couple in their kitchen, patching things up. That is where the movie left them, over a large meal, in the dark kitchen, their children growing up around them.

"I don't know why they have to be like that," Steve said on the way out.

"Like what?" Ginny asked, although she had wondered too.

"All full of misery. God knows, the people I know aren't like that."

"Probably not. It all works out, though, in the end, doesn't it?"

"I suppose."

Without two cars they would never have managed five years of twice a week. Now he solemnly opened her door and helped her in and patted her on the shoulder. Then like a little parade they drove away toward dinner.

The Four Elms had once been a speakeasy. Then it became a family restaurant. Behind it was a pond in which a family of ducks swam, waiting for dinner. In front of it were the two remaining elms and a parking lot full of Buicks. All day Sunday families waited in line for free tables, all the men turning their hat brims round and round in their hands, their wives, who wore little furs over their silk dresses, talking to each other. The children and grandchildren threw stones at the ducks. When the tables were free, they took off their overcoats and hung up their furs, read through the menu and ordered the day's special, which for Sunday was veal cutlets and spaghetti. And these people were good eaters; they had all been to church that morning and had taken the whole family for a drive up to Point of Firs. They had put on their best clothes, listened with worry to the sermon, given enough to the two collections, observed the speed laws, bought frozen custard for the children, and now they were eating the day's special.

Steve and Ginny pushed themselves up the waiting bench, speaking to men from the store and women from her office.

When the waiter asked, "What'll it be, Steve?" he answered:
"Two cutlets, and bring me a beer and the little lady a coke."
He did. They ate slowly, talking about the movie, remaking
the lives of the characters so that they would not have been
killed and orphaned. Their benches were set back to back
with other couples'. Behind Steve's, Ginny saw an almost
identical head, gray in the same spots, heavy jawed. At her
back, she heard a voice encouraging children to eat everything on their plates and a bracelet jangling as it rose and
fell.

Always when it was over, they waited after the dessert as
if something was going to happen. Then Steve collected
his change and they said good night to everybody they would
see in the morning. In the parking lot he unlocked her car,
held the door open, and patted her shoulder again.

"Wednesday, huh?" he said.

She hesitated a moment and said: "Sure, Wednesday."

THERE WON'T

BE ANY

SCARS AT ALL

⋞⧏⧐⋟ Looking into his face, everyone felt suddenly old. Hearing his voice, people were reminded of youth and freedom they imagined that they once had.

Every September the rest of the faculty slunk back to the college ashamed of their misspent summers, wretched about having done nothing but watch July and August wither. Into this depressed area glittered that perennially golden boy-professor, Stanley Pious, fresh from Dar Es Salaam, Montevideo, or Baffin Island with another sackful of strange rocks and a year's worth of quaint anecdotes: Dr. Stanley Pious, assistant professor of geology, indispensable older brother to every girl in the college.

His faculty colleagues sat behind their closed office doors waiting for it to be time to go home or to their lectures, fearing that the young steps creaking up the stairway and down the corridor of the Earth Sciences Building might be for them. But smelling their worry, the student looking for their signature on an IBM card would be blessedly brief and impersonal, in and out of the office within three minutes. If the student had other problems, she solved them by taking LSD or a junior year in Kyoto or lying on the couch of the one-legged Dr. Alyce-Mae Peabody, college psychiatrist.

How differently the confident fans of Stanley Pious charged up the stairs, and seeing the waiting line, sighed, and putting their spines to the wall, sank down to wait. Two or three lucky early arrivals inside that magic door were loudly analyzing their adolescences or diagnosing the diseases of dormitory living. A couple of times a semester older faculty members made a curious inspection of the corridor, trying to glance into that office without seeming to, and there cross-legged on the desk like an athletic Buddha sat Dr. Stanley Pious, guru and confessor.

To older colleagues, even those younger than he, he was elaborately polite, for which they alternately respected and hated him. In his judgment they were all muddling into decadent middle age anyway, while he worked out in the gym every afternoon, skied through the spring, surfed all summer, climbed impressive little mountains in the fall, and won a black belt at judo. He was a walking treasury of large and small skills, could tell the weather from bird flights, knew how to exorcise an incubus, was rumored to be able to read Minoan A, and turned out a great home brew for 2½ cents a glass. Of course, he wrote an elegant italic hand and with his hand press printed abstract Christmas cards on rice paper.

In the midst of these glittering accomplishments he sat

surprised and humble, listening to the troubles of the young with as much intensity as if he had never had school, parents, love, or marriage to contend with. Actually, he had emerged unscathed from contact with all of them. The students would never believe that he had ever been a human baby or had sat at a greasy desk in a dusty high school homeroom, but scraps of Stanley Pious's biography were circulated by those garrulous academic historians, the publishers' representatives and the departmental secretaries. At conventions and symposia in the faceless rooms of giant hotels, the bills paid for by the colleges at which they taught, geologists or physicists or oceanographers sat around in the late evenings unpeeling the real (or was it?) Stanley Pious.

He had grown up in one of the consistently ugly cities of the Northeast and recognized the dimensions of its ugliness long before urban planners stripped away thousands of decayed tenements, ramshackle groceries, and miles of used-car lots—finding at the end that there had been nothing worth saving at all. It was erroneous to call something blighted that had never been healthy. In his childhood walks along the cracked pavements and past the back doorways in which crocheted eagles spread themselves over the window glass, Stanlet plotted his escape and considered the greatest human possessions—which were money, good taste, youth, thinness, and a camel's-hair coat.

His route toward good taste was directly paved through jobs as caddy and cabana boy at a resort so old and rich that the clubhouse was screened with decaying bottle-green lattice work, and all the plumbing dated from 1904. From these summers he learned to buy one very good sports jacket from Abercrombie's rather than a two-pants suit from Robert Hall, and two white camellias rather than a carnation corsage when he took the dull girls from good families to school dances.

His grandparents and parents had been named Piouskow-ski, but some wit in Stanley's fourth grade had run to the blackboard when the nun was out of the room for a moment and had drawn there a cartoon of a fat Jersey, eyes turned toward heaven, devout front hooves clasped, while its great rear knelt at a flimsy *prie-dieu*. It was labeled "Stanley, the praying cow." That was one of the reasons he had abbreviated the Piouskowski.

The other legend described his marriage in graduate school to a professor's daughter; people remembered her as bonily handsome, given to cashmere sweaters and monogrammed gold barrettes holding back her flat blond hair. Stories conflicted on Stanley's strategy in marrying her. Perhaps he simply decided that her family provided a cut-rate ticket into the academic world. Her father was a gracious party-giving department chairman, whose office had custom-woven draperies and an Oriental. Her mother looked like Ginger Rogers but cooked like somebody's Hungarian grandmother and laughed in a rich explosive scale as she shoved platters of gravy-soaked mashed potatoes, pork pies, and puff pastries toward the hungry and uncertain graduate students.

Who would have guessed that the father-in-law would be fired loudly and lengthily on a coed's charge of improper conduct during a fraternity brawl, that he would find a job nowhere and run through his savings in a year, that he would join his daughter and Stan in their four-room apartment, or that the mother-in-law would forget how to cook in favor of crying with as much gusto as she had formerly spent laughing. That was not at all what Stan had married, so when their fraud infected his dream, he simply cleared out— took his Burberry, his good jacket, his handmade shirts, and two buckram atlases from his father-in-law's library and went to Europe. Here the legend is somewhat dim. The professor's daughter, never notably imaginative, did realize after the first year that Stan was not on a cruise, so she went out and found a job as a kindergarten teacher. As far as Stan was concerned, she never happened.

If he had encountered colds, late trains, bad meals, chilblains, roaches, or dysentery, nobody could tell when he drove his Triumph off the dock with the completed thesis and two brocade vests in the luggage compartment. That was about five years ago, the stage at which he began growing younger.

He was a natural for the faculty of a girls' college. Hostesses, delighted simply by an extra man, were overwhelmed that he knew how to carve the duck and flame the crêpes. The administration was impressed by the deferential stance he assumed before anyone over twenty-one and by his energy. Whenever they looked through the glass doors into his laboratory, he was not simply walking from bench to bench: he ran, arched, bent, leapt, gestured as if the rocks might be expected to follow direction. At faculty meetings he seemed as bug-eyed as he might have been at a tennis match, watch-

ing the faces and occasionally writing something on a memo
pad, deciding his vote slowly on the basis of the apparent
wish of the dean.

"The new man"—he was called the new man for several
years—"doesn't seem to have much time for bridge, does
he?" Henry Farber, who taught psychology, commented to
his wife. Since it was cheap and got no one into trouble,
bridge was the big thing at the college and all the faculty tried
to outdo each other by learning new tricks. That was why
the library had such a huge games collection. Henry Farber
was the dean of the bridge players; he devoted himself so
single-mindedly to it that teaching and Mrs. Farber and the
kids had become incidental. To Stanley Pious bridge was
in the same category as bubble gum, bingo, bowling, drive-in
movies, and coon-dogs.

"It's funny. You think you have Stanley in conversation,"
Henry Farber went on, "but you really don't. I mean, he's
standing directly in front of you and asking you questions
every time there's a silence, but he isn't listening to a word
you're saying. His eyes are weaving around the room and a
clock inside his skull is counting the minutes until freedom."

Helen Farber, whose mental processes were as subtle as an
earthworm's, impulsively put her arm through his on the way
to the door after dinner one evening and said: "You're wonderful to have stayed as long as you did tonight, Stanley."
She was full of gratitude for the incredible patience this poor
dear new young man had expended in sacrificing himself
through the tedious night. "I suppose," she ended, "that
your night is just beginning now."

It became the fashion to discover women who might help Stan through the ordeals of these evenings, and several women were imported for this purpose. Most of them were contemporaries of his hostesses, dutiful to their responsibilities as guests, and accomplished game-players. They could describe the eastern face of Mt. Washington, play the cello, make rose hip jam, imitate Greta Garbo, cure ham, and mix a fine martini. They made money in textile designing, or had been involved in Mississippi voter registration, or pointed out high and low pressure areas on TV weather shows or flew their own planes. Stanley Pious, dazzlingly tailored, turned his face toward the clever lady of that week, begged pardon for his early departure, and stalked away without remembering her name.

"Well," Helen Farber said, shutting the door behind him. "It's not worth the effort. We ought to leave him alone. His interests must lie elsewhere." Released from feeling guilty about Stan, they liked him much better, and freed from their Saturday night bridge dinners, he smiled and waved at their passing cars.

It was evident that he belonged entirely to the students who invited him to Sunday brunches in dormitories and for a glass of beer in the town tavern. For several semesters, while the faculty played bridge, the students had been favoring discussion as their favorite indoor sport. So, in an Aran knit sweater matching his eyes, Stan crouched in the center of a great circle of them discussing Orphan Annie, American colonialism, Fanny Hill, Ingmar Bergman, or—very rarely—what we should do when all the petroleum dries up.

"You know, his lectures are so fascinating," the freshmen bubbled to older listeners, "that it doesn't seem to be geology at all." And they were likely to remark to him: "We never think of you as a geologist."

In the autumn of his fifth year at the college, Stanley became the uneasy object of an intense pursuit by Charlotte Mandell, who was a transfer student that fall. People wondered where he first became aware of her. Was she in a trenchcoat scuffing up Latin Way behind him in the fallen maple leaves or leaning forward on the writing arm of her first-row seat in the natural science auditorium, biting the eraser of her pencil and staring openly at him?

She was a big natural-looking girl who made you think of the good life in small towns surrounded by wheat fields. Actually, she had grown up in Pittsburgh, and her family was genuinely and unrepentantly rich. She was born with that terrible and wonderful trait of absolute honesty, and never sensed how rare it is. If you took the trouble, she was sure, you would find that everyone else was basically honest too.

"Who is that pretty girl who is always sitting in Stanley Pious's car?" Helen Farber asked her husband.

She might as well have asked the refrigerator. Henry glanced at girls as if they were billboards written in Chinese characters. In one of his rare indications of taste, he had once remarked after the evening news that he really found Queen Juliana an unusually attractive woman.

But having little to do, he found out and reported Charlotte's name, which seemed to give Helen Farber the right to smile and wave as if they were accomplices, which in a way

they were. The faculty wives then wondered why they had
not thought of serving up students rather than their own
interesting women friends during the Stanley Pious-party-giv-
ing stage. The wives tended to forget the students entirely,
preferring to pretend that their husbands went off at odd
hours of the day to offices where they sat behind a console
of telephones or signed contracts involving millions of dollars
or invited cronies to make up a golf foursome.

Within a few weeks Charlotte had learned what Stanley
liked and set about donating a dazzling series of gifts in
return for an occasional dinner. How could Stanley ignore
them—cufflinks crafted by a Danish silversmith from a
Belgium reliquary, a twentieth share in a two-year-old racing
in the Preakness, a bound set of Batman comic books, a hunk
of gold ore caught in lucite. He coveted all these and the expectation of many more too much to ask the price or to
look out the office window at the battered station wagons
filled with waiting wives and kiddies who might be a sign of
the future.

Helen Farber and all the wives were campaigning for Charlotte. To their picnics she brought white boxes tied with wide
ribbons in which were sacher torte and petits fours. Their
children insisted that she looked like Rima the bird girl except that she played hopscotch too well.

"You're so wonderful. We know you can make Stanley
happy," Helen confided to her in the kitchen when they were
all a little tight at a party given for a famous astronomer who
was then standing in the middle of the Farber's living room
pretending to be a falling meteor.

"I'm not sure at all," Charlotte confessed. "Of course, I'm completely in love with him, which, I guess, is perfectly obvious to everyone but Stanley. But I seem to be just one of the crowd of admirers. Even when we're alone, it's as if there were lots of other people there and he were talking to them."

Swaying over the ice bucket, Helen tried to slide two cubes into her glass. "I think you've caught him. There are signs that he will finally marry and settle down with us."

"You really think so?" Charlotte would have delightedly believed any of Helen's fantasies, but the meteor expert swished into the kitchen with loud demands for more ice, and the moment was lost.

Stanley Pious was about as ready for marriage as J. Edgar Hoover. He had nothing against Charlotte. She would make someone a good wife, and he wished that the someone would find her soon. Although in Helen Farber's cozy imagination they were engaged, he had never made a single promise beyond Saturday night dinner. For Christmas, without telling a soul, he flew to Quebec while Charlotte searched for him at the geologists' convention. When he returned, the waiting lines of fans were even longer outside his office, stimulated by the possibility that he might be in love and they could find this emotion etched on his face. Charlotte borrowed her father's Jaguar to follow the Triumph along the icy back roads; when her parents arranged for him to spend a long weekend at their Palm Beach house, he pleaded off on the excuse of writing an article. In his determination to free himself before the net settled, he spent his weekends traveling but was running out of places to go. His tension, he could see, was making him far less amusing to the other girls than he used to be.

That spring was unusually wet. The gritty snowdrifts shriveled into little ponds. Over the slate roofs, down the gutters, along the soggy paths, into the spongy earth, it drizzled and poured. Chalk refused to write and clothes never seemed to dry. In the distance heavy crows drifted tiredly. The campus turned black and gray; the sides of granite buildings, the mossy trunks of elms, the wrought-iron fences, the bicycle racks, were all stained darker than in winter. After the first sodden week everyone was nervously resentful of the streaming window panes and the foggy edges of the day. The girls refused to go to classes or to read or even to visit Stanley; they played dozens of hands of bridge, watched daytime TV, and ate pizza.

In the late afternoon of one of these days which had not had a proper morning or noon but had remained in foggy suspension for several hours, Charlotte appeared at the door of Stanley's office. She was wearing a green silk cape, and her face was unsmiling. He was, for once, almost too tired to talk but grabbed the first impersonal topic he could think of to fight off the silence. He had heard this folk rock song on the car radio; the tune was a lot like "A Worried Man," but the words were ambiguous enough to refer to an ordinary salesman or a drug addict or a pacifist. Had she heard the song? She was standing with her back to him staring into a case of rock samples, but he miserably accepted the fact that he could not interest her in quaint anecdotes or small talk, and she was probably crying. He was about to tell her that it was the weather that was making everyone nervous. Did she know the effects of cyclones, typhoons, tornadoes, monsoons, of the mistral—upon various populations? In the middle of what, he thought, was a promising lecture, she whirled around, and she was, indeed, crying. He wondered if he should offer his handkerchief or pretend not to notice, but that would have been ridiculous. He would be direct.

"Charlotte, don't be upset. You're not in love with me. You only think you are. Many years from now if you can remember this spring, the whole affair will seem impossible. What's really wrong is this damned rain. Naturally it affects personality. You're going to feel entirely different in the summer. You could fly down to Bermuda right now. Why don't you do that."

She was crying too fiercely to be able to speak clearly. She seemed to be shouting, but her voice by the time it got by the sobbing was hard to understand. "That's all you care? I love you enough to die, and that's all you care? I suppose you're bored with hearing girls say they love you. Do you tell all of them to fly away somewhere? Or do you tell them it's the rain or the sun that's the problem and then try to entertain them with jokes or card tricks? Oh, you're right. If I wait long enough, I'll forget. If I wait long enough, I'll be dead."

He was glad that she had become angry. Not only did it minimize his guilt, but it gave him the right to be angry too. Many girls had cried in the office before over grades, parents, life, themselves, but none over him.

"Now go away," he said. "Eat dinner and have a good sleep. You look very tired. We can talk again some other time."

That seemed to make no difference. "You want me to go away. You really want me to go far away?"

"I only want you to eat dinner and then get to work on some of the term papers you must have. Isn't it almost time for dinner anyway?"

"I suppose it is." She was still crying. He was suddenly very tired of her. He had not invited her to crawl inside the cave of his heart and point her flashlight at the walls. He had patterned a fine, really an enviable, life that was being threatened. On his desk were the talismans of that life—invitations for weekends, rocks from friendly beaches, a gossipy letter from his old thesis advisor, a brochure describing next summer's trip up the Amazon.

He pretended to be busy with a stack of lab exercises and in a moment or so he heard her say, "I'm going," and she did. Her scudding footfall echoed through the empty hallway and down the stairs; the outside door slammed, and she was standing on the porch deciding what pathway to take. The Earth Sciences Building, like most of the departmental offices, was in a Victorian house the college had bought a few years before and painted inside and out with a shade of cream that faded to mud. All the rooms—kitchen, pantry, parlor—were now offices. Stanley's must have been the front bedroom. He had put andirons in the fireplace and driftwood on the mantel and painted the walls white and hung up maps and an abstraction which the artist, a friend of his, said was a portrait of him. It was called "Solitary Man Waiting for the Sound of Time." In the late afternoon, these office buildings seemed to become old houses again, and if you stayed in them long enough, you began to imagine screen doors banging and voices in the kitchen among the clatter of supper dishes. Stanley took the lab exercises and drove back to his apartment. He was a much better cook than most of the worried faculty wives.

While he was taking a shower the next morning, he congratulated himself on how well he had handled the situation with Charlotte. There were times when encouragement could do a great deal of harm.

By his first class the drizzle had stopped and the sun began to freshen the dankest corners of the rain-stained walls and walks. On the pavements were maple keys or the remains of the delicate flowers that most serious trees wear for a few spring days. Charlotte was not at the lecture, and the fact that she had taken his sensible advice and probably gone on a trip, the good weather, the clean breeze at the open window, were enough to encourage Stanley through what must have been a fine discussion of some Paleozoic ledges.

After the lecture a knot of particular favorites always stood around the lectern or sat on the chair arms waiting to walk toward the coffee shop with him.

"Isn't it awful about Charlotte?" one asked.

"What about her?"

"She cut her wrists last night. We thought you knew."

It is all some kind of undergraduate joke, he thought. She has put them up to this. She wants me to suffer and has coached them in this story and is now waiting in my office.

"Where is she?" he asked.

"The infirmary. She came into Julie's room about midnight looking like a tragic heroine and told us to call a doctor. But we thought that no doctor would come to a dormitory in the middle of the night so we put some towels over her arms and drove her to the infirmary. The night nurse is a real goon. I mean *she* went out of her mind, as if she'd never seen human blood before and it looked as if we'd have to tie her up in a corner and fetch Peg-leg Peabody."

"What about Charlotte?"

"She's all right, I guess. It was probably just some kind of accident. She wasn't hysterical and they weren't really deep cuts."

He searched their clear eyes. It might have been their first reaction to blame someone, but they had trained themselves never to judge categorically. They would argue the case for several weeks, then shrug their shoulders and dismiss it as a private matter. They did expect some reaction from him.

Thinking of himself, he said: "Why, that's perfectly horrible news."

A grim newsreel of the incident jerked in his mind: Charlotte crying in the dark office, Charlotte frightened, holding out thick reddening toweled stumps, Charlotte explaining to the listeners, to the deans, to her parents, he telling the dean, "My relationship with Miss Mandell was, of course, entirely proper," the dean's disbelief, the papers, the talk, and a flashback to his almost-forgotten once-father-in-law saying about the coed who had accused him: "I never laid a hand on her."

"I must visit her," he said.

"Yes, you can visit her in the afternoon," they said, "from three to five."

"Aren't you coming for coffee?" they asked. It was not that they were heartless or patronizing. They had grown up in a world where people ate their dinners while watching flood, riot, and bombing between the dog food commercials on evening TV.

"No," he said, "I'm not going for coffee today. I must grade some papers."

The sunlight outside annoyed him. He imagined old faculty members hunched behind their office windows staring down at him, glad that undergraduates did not notice them, glad that they had become gray nonentities, glad that he had finally got what he deserved. They will fire me, he thought. As soon as they realize that she killed herself—or tried to—over me. At scientific meetings I will overhear two of them in a lobby or an elevator enjoying my story. If trapped into talking to me, they will be light-hearted and compulsively remind me how liberal the college is. If it weren't for the publicity, they will say, you could have stayed here forever, but with the world outside as it is, you've outlived your usefulness here, don't you see? How long would they remember? How far would he have to go? He saw himself teaching general science in a nonaccredited seminary in Montana—no, a seminary wouldn't have him—perhaps a business college in Juneau, on the second floor, over a loan company and a dentist. Or glad of a job with British Petroleum in Kuwait, he would walk out onto the porch at a Polo Club dance and there among the palms hear a new arrival from the States describing how Stanley Pious was kicked out of teaching.

He waited the rest of the morning and early afternoon for

the summons to the president or the dean, but none came. Girls came, a few of them mentioned Charlotte, and his mask was moved by some old reflexes. He felt that his real self had crawled out of the bone box and was crouched, shrunken to the size of a rock specimen in the glass case, watching himself laugh and giggle and pout and mug his way through the hours of girls.

He wondered how the older men who taught with him would show their scorn. On the pretext of going to the supply room, he passed their offices and stared into them but could see nothing strange in any of their faces except for mild surprise at Stanley Pious wandering the corridors. I could rush shouting my guilt into the faculty dining room where all the neat gray-haired spinsters are fiddling with their place mats, and they would all have a chance to gasp at the nasty young man. This is the way mad heroes of old Russian novels behaved, he thought, and what is my guilt anyway? If today were yesterday, I would not change a word.

At three o'clock he rang the doorbell at the infirmary and explained to the tight-lipped nurse that he had come to see Miss Mandell. The nurse was, he guessed, treating him with the same skepticism she showed the overwrought girls who reported strange noises in their heads and spasms in their tendons. She disapproved of higher education for women, saw mononucleosis, if it existed, as a response to pent-up sexual energy. None of them, she thought, exercised enough or washed enough. It was no wonder with such disorderly lives that they needed tranquilizers, took dope, slit their wrists.

"I'll tell her you're here," she snapped.

He waited in the lounge. It was supposed to be a jolly, sun-lit place. Actually the glare made his eyes water and his head reel. The nurse squished back.

"All right. You can come now. She's in room ten."

There seemed to be no one else in the whole infirmary. He walked cautiously lest his fear spill out of his body.

In a blue wool bathrobe, Charlotte was sitting beside the window reading a book. Her hair was pulled back from her face as she wore it on occasions of seriousness, exams, before weekends she spent at home, yesterday in the office. Though he tried to keep his eyes fixed on her face, they dropped to her wrists; on the insides were strips of adhesive little larger than Band-Aids. She closed the book and stared at him. Of course, he had expected her to be a green-skinned wraith, tearful against the pillow, hurling insults, and wearing the marks of some great struggle. Instead, she waved him to a chair as if she were a strong-willed widow skillfully running her late husband's business and Stanley Pious were a rather tedious client who had to be put up with.

"I am awfully sorry," he said, "if I had anything to do with it."

"*If* you did?" she asked ironically. "Originally, I thought you had everything to do with it, but I learned better. When you threw me out of the office yesterday I despised you. I could have torn you apart and thrown your head into a fish-bowl to feed my guppies. I wanted to scratch some of the veneer off of you to see what was underneath."

"I was very concerned when I heard about you this morning."

"Don't interrupt. I have to tell you a few things. You were concerned—how typical. You were concerned about whether somebody killed herself and about whether you should tip a headwaiter and about whether you can wear your brown jacket once more before you send it to the cleaner's. I spent some time last night reflecting on your concerns, and I reached the conclusion that all of them are too small to be seen with the naked eyes."

"I'm sorry you hate me so much."

"I don't hate you at all. This is a kind of expensive way to find out that I don't care one way or the other about you. I suppose you thought I tried to kill myself because you sent me away, and I suppose it started with self-pity."

"You wanted to make me suffer a little too, didn't you?"

"And just how could I have made you suffer?"

"Why, they would have fired me. I would have been done for in this business. Don't you realize how I would have been hurt?"

"I'm the patient, remember? If you're afraid I'm going to involve you in this affair, forget it. Clever young Dr. Pious is quite safe. The foolish young woman is removing herself from the premises. Everything will be exactly as it was before." She looked down at her wrists. "And there won't be any scars at all."

He was almost obviously jubilant. "I still don't understand why you did it."

"Nor do I. At the moment I scraped this arm, I began to think of the really decent people like my parents and my kid sister whom I never appreciated enough. And then I thought how lucky I was and how I wanted to wake up the next morning. That's why I ran for help immediately, and it's a funny thing, I haven't thought of you since then."

The nurse appeared at the door, indicating that he had been there too long.

"Good-bye," she said, returning to her book.

He walked out, thinking: She's putting on a good act. I'm glad I didn't behave rashly.

DIVORCING

THE DEAD

HUSBAND

❧❧❧ A year after Fred Ryan married Lillian Whitford, he drove into the trunk of a seventy-five-year-old oak tree on Route 105 at seven o'clock on a Thursday evening in October, and from the oak tree bounced across the road through a highway fence into a trench below. The side of the tree trunk was gouged and its bark shredded; the rubber skid marks punctuated the road for a couple of months. Fred's body crouched beneath the steering wheel; Lillian, almost unscratched, lay ten feet from the jagged windshield.

Two years before, she had told Fred, "My life is very quiet, really like a millpond," and he had warned, "You know, I'm not the most exciting man in the world," and that was the way they proposed to each other. When the bride's over forty, and it's the husband's second marriage, there aren't the surprises. The man and woman are pretty much all they're going to be. If she squeezes the toothpaste tube in the middle and snores, both are beyond correction. The stamp of the next twenty years is there for the watcher with any imagination. He will lose more hair, and his nose and chin will take up more space. Their digestions will get worse. People hearing of their wedding will be amused or will say: "Well, there's a comfortable couple, now." And everyone will know almost everything and at the same time nothing about them.

When Lillian was young, she dreamed of marrying a blind man, but knowing none, she waited for the less needy to notice that she needed them.

"There is always someone." Her mother was positive. "You have only to work to be seen."

"It's your face," a friend announced. "It's kind of off-center isn't it or something? I don't see it any more, for looking at you all these years, but new people"—by which she meant men—"might be put off."

And her father, frail in the afternoon sunporch, clasped her hand in his shaky claw: "You're a good-looking woman, like your grandmother." But he was commenting on her voice, and her pushing the wheelchair into the sun, and gliding into the room when he coughed at night.

Why Fred married her was never clear to Lillian but it had something to do with his first wife. He had his daughter Hallie, married and away but more efficient as a consequence, a cleaning woman twice a week, and someone else who made a week's worth of dinners and left them with the heating-up instructions. He had all the consolations of work, church, grandchildren, a nonpainful heart condition, gardening, and cursing the water lilies in the pond in front of the house that snagged and chewed the fishing lines.

His first wife, Phyllis, never let people go. She wrote let-ters to names in the full address book, although she could not remember the faces or voices matching them. She tran-scribed all the vital information into the address book. Birth-day and anniversary cards convinced people she had met at conventions or sat next to on the train to New York that they had shared a moment of great significance. And Fred and she spent Sundays visiting those left, as she said, "wandering these shores after tragedy has struck." One of the latter was her old business-school chum, Lillian Whitford. Not that Lil-lian had encountered any experience worthy of being called a tragedy: her parents slipped away on a regular and well-defined passage to the other side.

Aside from caring for Ma and Pa, who could have been said to care far more for her, Lillian worked in the office of a lumber company, really ran the company, could rhapsodize over three-inch plank from British Columbia and possible combinations of Chinese red and antique green latex paint, if anyone wanted to hear. She loved the smell of newly planed wood and bins of grass seed. Above the lumberyard in a glassed-in office like a train dispatcher's, she did prodigious amounts of work in a day, the windows open, the shades flapping in the wind, the roll-top desk rattling as the old Remington invoiced, thanked, dunned, explained. She was cheerful about her parents' decay in the way some-one might be who had discovered that the world was not really a place in which to live but a hospital in which to prepare for death—which, after all, lasted long enough to be worth long contemplation.

After the parents had made the trip to the other side,

Phyllis said, "We must have Lillian here," and they had her and she had them, back and forth, pretending they had a lot to say to each other, but it was mostly preparing to go and come. The carrying of suitcases and meeting of trains and writing of thank-yous made the visits seem more impressive than they were.

Lillian's family had been dimly Methodist. Fred and Phyllis were Roman Catholics, the kind that simply assumed, politely, that everyone else was, too. Once Lillian had asked, "What's Heaven like, Phyl?" who had without hesitation answered, "Everybody sitting around, dressed simply, you know, everybody—all the people we know—talking and, I suppose eating occasionally and beautiful music and happiness."

"Everybody, Phyl?"

"Well, I suppose some have to suffer a while. I don't like to think about that."

They were not belongers. So few in the town were that the K. of C., the Daughters of Isabella, the Holy Name, like the Odd Fellows, and the Moose, were skeletal. They met seldom. The odd members shifted offices among themselves and wondered how much longer they could maintain their drafty lodges. The Ryans' parish church, renovated within an inch of its life, had stopped having suppers and bazaars and had substituted second collections. The parish priest lived with his skinny sister inside the monumental rectory with a lot of varnish, shellac, wall-to-wall dark-brown broadloom, and a tapestry of the Last Supper, which Father Morrissey had bought at an Indianapolis Confraternity Convention. He had grown up in the next town, where there were relatives who called him Father John and old men who remembered his father, the fire chief. So there was not much mystery to Father Morrissey, who wouldn't, anyway, have known what to do with it. His style had been given him in his youth: he was a friendly priest, great smile, bigger laugh, large hands always waving, glittering glasses, a sense of cleanliness and health, except that he smoked too much and had trouble giving it up for Lent. Every morning he walked down-street at ten to pick up the papers and at eight at night in cassock he locked the church. If trapped into a conversation on either occasion, he favored the weather and sports; he was said to be close to children and the very old. He waved up at the Ryans' front porch where on Saturdays Fred, on his day off from the store, sat between Phyl and Lillian. Lillian was now asked for almost every weekend.

Phyl continued to observe to Lillian: "Migsy likes you." Migsy was a bright-eyed, cinnamon-colored chow with an irritated single bark she addressed to almost everyone except Lillian. One should not really make a future from a dog's acceptance or a series of weekends or the cheery threesome being waved at by Father Morrissey, but Fred did.

During Phyl's long sickness in the hospital, Lillian visited there regularly. Although she seldom cried about anything, she had cried when Phyllis spent an hour peeling an orange and then was too tired to eat it. The orange rolled off the bed and splatted on the floor. Lillian winced as she picked it up, and went into the corridor to cry where aides were filling bowls with cream soup for supper.

Six months later, when Fred asked her to marry him, she remembered the dusty orange and Phyllis's uncoordinated hand and the chipped bed, and agreed instantly. Some experiences, perhaps, give you a right to spend the rest of your life with someone. Primitive people are tied by stranger similarities: the angle the sun slants over a straw roof or the way a bird flies.

"Will the children mind?" she asked him. There were two, Ben and Hallie.

"What business is it of theirs? They have their own lives now."

After he had proposed and gone home, she dared to telephone, wondering if it were true.

"You're not busy?"

"Goodness, no, Lil. Glad to hear from you."

"I wanted to ask what I should buy."

Silence clutched the wire. Then he asked: "The house doesn't need anything, does it?"

"I suppose not."

In the lonely reaches of furniture departments, among the orphaned beds and chairs and at the edges of the smart, make-believe rooms, she sighed. If she bought even one chair, the house would open and become like others, which Fred would not permit. Downstairs in the store, a faintly pink-haired girl flashed hands delicate enough to break under net peignoirs. She was showing what she would buy, and looked with sad scorn at Lillian's choice. "Sensible," she said.

At the wedding, Lillian wore a blue lace dress and sat in the front seat between Hallie and her husband on the drive to the church. She felt less experienced than the squirming grandchildren scratching their white socks and hitting their patent leather shoes against the back of her seat. They met Ben and Fred in the parking lot beside the church and self-consciously hurried inside the sacristy of St. Joseph's. It was a late Sunday afternoon in October. Beyond loomed the great, musty church, wearing a sour smell of sixty years of overshoes and candles. The sacristy was layers of yellow varnish and closets of vestments from which Father Morrissey put on a white surplice. He bent, speaking politely to her, being careful to smile. "The bride's nervous, isn't she? This is the time to run out. Last warning."

She always wondered if the Ryans and the people they knew would behave differently if she were not there. Would they wear other expressions? Would they shout and rant? Everyone in the sacristy was bent on hiding the purpose of the event by hanging a veil between the fact and their fears.

"You'll just stand in front of me and read the responses from this book," Father Morrissey told her, and they filed into the dark church, Lillian tightly clasping the book, the neat children hidden in a front pew, Hallie and Ben on either side of Fred and herself.

"Not until we get outside," Hallie warned the children, who later threw handfuls of confetti which fell over and between the wet cobblestones and darkened among the bright leaves that had dropped in the rain that afternoon. Fred and Lillian walked carefully toward the car. Hallie had arranged with a caterer to serve supper to twenty or thirty people who might become friends, and who spoke together what they were expected to say: "Wonderful, lovely, just like a bride, happy, good luck, just great, fine, that's the stuff, let's have a toast, look this way, what a wonderful day, now the fun begins, let's have a kiss, I can't tell you how happy we were when we heard, Fred looks proud as a peacock, wonder how you'll like being a housewife?" The women had had their hair done; they wore stoles, silk flowered dresses and heavy perfume, and many of them vaguely rubbed a cheek against hers. Their husbands, sure that all women were the same, kissed her on the lips.

In the evening, they drove away on what they called "the trip." What surprised her most about love was how brief it was. Standing in her dressing gown at the window of the motel, she watched Fred polishing the car, intently examining something he must have thought looked like a scratch on the finish. Also, there was nothing to say about it: the memory might throb and burn in the head, but the lips opened to talk only about breakfast and the newspaper. She was amazed that love left no marks. Others would sleep in the same bed that night without knowing them, and some day the old walls of the motel would be pulled down by fire or wreckers and no trace of their stay would exist.

The first year, she told herself, will be like a laboratory exercise, a practical examination which I must not fail. When they returned from the trip, it was Halloween. The children of the area knew their part of the show and thumped boldly or cautiously into the living room, dragged sacks almost as tall as they were. Fred pretended horror over and over, shielding his eyes, widening his mouth, hiding behind the winged chair, cautioning the smallest elves against goblins, giving their mothers trick-or-treat bags for the babies at home. Lillian opened and closed the door for the marauding gangs of kids, sure that she had seen the same ones five times. Once she asked a tall boy with rouged cheeks and a red satin evening dress who he was, and he giggled violently. "Just some dame."

"He always wants to dress up in his sister's clothes," the mother said dotingly. She might have been describing his 4-H project, his plans for college.

He put his candy bar gracefully into his sequined bag.

"You certainly make a fine girl," Fred said, bowing courteously.

"What happened to you?" Lillain asked a sobbing Indian.

"He keeps hitting me on the head. My brother, that's Daniel Boone, is always trying to kill me."

The brother again attempted to scalp him. "Another redskin hits the dust," Fred announced cheerily.

"He's really bleeding a lot. Shouldn't we call his mother?"

"Good for him. Toughen him up. It's all in fun."

After the bleeding Indian there were girls in space suits, bellies swollen by pillows into pregnancies; a skeleton carrying its skull. A spindly kid, who fit perfectly into his father's World War II Eisenhower jacket, was collecting his candy in a German helmet. Lillian was pursued by horrors too obscure to name and by a headache that lacerated separate sections of her brain at the same time.

What would Phyllis have done? Lillian tried to remember

her, and was more shocked that she could not form a complete picture but got sections—gestures, her back, her hats, her shoes. Once she had told Lillian: "I look first at people's feet. You can tell a lot from the condition of their shoes, don't you think?" When talking, Phyllis often spread her fingers over her nose and eyes like a visor, as if what she were confiding were jokes or secrets. But she dealt in neither. She was monumentally positive about what she saw as life. Every question had its prefabricated answer. Asked what dentist she favored, she would tell how much her bridgework had cost. Mention convents as you passed one, she would announce, "Beggars," and launch into the history of her older sister, a nun for twenty-five years, who had left the convent two years ago and nobody had known about it until she called from a pay phone in the middle of one morning in March. Throw any name or noun into the air and Phyllis would slap it down with a single pronouncement. "Lawyers, robbers. Children: had to be shown who was boss. Catalpas: dirty trees. Bess Truman: a wonderful American. White cats: bad luck. Aspirin: thinned the blood. The Mass in English: a big mistake."

In the presence of the oracle, you nodded. Later, you remembered that catalpas are pretty in bloom and you had once happily loved a white cat.

If every abstraction in the world is indestructible, Lillian wondered where Phyllis's positiveness had gone. Was it caught in some closet? Running a finger over an embroidered bureau scarf or polishing a chair rung or staring at a chipped saucer in her hand, Lillian waited for the commanding voice. "Tell me what to do. By now you have seen me loose in this house. I am not what you and Fred intended. I am not what I intended, for that matter." Migsy, a faded shadow, moved painfully from room to room, and in her dull eyes there was no lesson. But no one mentioned Phyllis's name aloud. Magazines bearing her name on the subscription labels arrived, her metal box of recipes sat on the kitchen shelf, a patch of linoleum in front of the sink had been worn by her heels, but no one dared to say her name. Instead, Fred rearranged his sentences: "The house was always cleaned on Thursdays. Dinner got served usually around six. No one here liked horseradish—that's why there isn't any." One day he brought downstairs a large white box. "Here; it's never been worn. In the same box it came from the store." It was a mink stole, his last gift to Phyllis. On one Sunday, Hallie looked at the Portland vase Lillian had filled with lilacs. "They look nice. Too bad Mom never dared to use any of the Wedgwood." They watched Fred turn an angry profile and stalk away. Hallie never referred to her mother again.

The children charged through the house on Sundays. At the door, Hallie insisted, "You have kisses for Grandpa and Lillian," before they earned entrance. The family was misleading in touching and embracing as much as they did. There was a great quantity of hope in their rushing at each other, as if they might generate light and heat.

Lillian had lived alone long enough to be surprised by the noise, talk, and motion which sped the days. Fred was a noisy man; he reclaimed the house every morning by walking over as much of its surface as possible and touching the rest.

He pushed the calendar ahead with announcements: "We have to order the Christmas cards. We have to get them printed up."

"Couldn't we just get a lot of different ones and sign them?"

"No, people compare. They have to be the same. And the store party, don't forget that."

"What do the women wear?"

"All dressed up—very fancy. Some people dance after the dinner. It's a nice affair. You'll like it. At least most people do."

She went to buy the nice dress and tried on a black crepe with low back. The clerk arched her head at the view in the fitting-room mirror. "You can cover up the moles on your back with a nice flesh-colored make-up. No one'll know."

So she bought a red velvet with high neck.

When they reached the Cortez Room the night of the party, wives were standing over the buffet tables, poking at platters and chafing-dishes, dredging up the lobster chunks from the newburg and turning over the slices to the rarest pieces of roast beef. Amid the variety of food, what struck Lillian was the similarity of its taste. The vegetables and meat, fish and dessert, might all have been taken from the same vats and molded and colored into carrots, beans, turkey, and plum pudding.

"Great, isn't it?" Having said that, no one ate much of the high mounds of food on the plates. They hung over each other's chairs or made trips to the bar.

In the ladies' room, Lillian found a fat-faced woman hanging onto a washbowl and staring into the mirror. She was crying with abandon; tears dripped from her chin and spotted her garnet dress. Her mascara had run, giving the impression of two sets of eyes.

"None of you appreciate me," she cried. "I'm beautiful. I dress up and nobody talks to me. I'm prettier than any girl out there in this whole place. I shouldn't give the time of day to you creeps, not that much . . ." She tried to snap her fingers, but could not bring them together. In the process, she lost hold of the washbowl and slipped toward Lillian, who felt the stranger's wet face against her shoulder. She was at the same time embarrassed and fascinated. The woman slid to the floor, sitting among the scattered paper towels with lipstick blots and the combed-out hairs. "Damn you," the woman shouted, "you're laughing just like the rest. Don't you see? I'm beautiful." Lillian left her.

Outside at the Conquistadores Bar, Fred said: "I guess I'll have just one more pop."

A fuzzy girl with shaking bosom and thighs put her arm in his and ran her fingers coquettishly through her stiff hair. A shower of dandruff fell onto Fred's navy-blue shoulder. "Joannie works with me, you know, Lil. We think the world of each other. We'll all have another drink. What do you want, Lil?"

"Nothing," she answered. As he turned away, she knew that she had failed again. She was becoming egocentric enough to think that she was responsible for many things that were not her business at all—the crying woman and Joannie's dandruff. She made the evening miserable by shaking out her terrible worries before people trying to forget their own.

There was Christmas itself to be failed at, too. "Shouldn't we have the children?" she asked Fred.

"Oh, all right."

Hallie was positive about imposing limitation, as if she were dealing with international warfare. "They can't come until after the gifts here." Lillian could see her standing in the hallway of her distant house, holding the telephone while the trolls brayed their disapproval below. "After they open their presents here, we will come to you. Otherwise, chaos." When she used such telegraphic style, you were supposed to fill in the real horror, more than any concentration of weeks of real children could provide: tears of disappointment, throttling convulsions, upset stomachs, rocketing screams, tense threats, crashing furniture, decapitated dolls, writhing headaches scraping your bones, footsteps knocking against your spine. Hallie's idea of children was worse than any reality.

"Shouldn't we buy toys?" Lillian asked.

"Thursday night," Fred announced.

She parked near the store in expectation of great armfuls of successful buys. "Would they like stuffed animals?" She touched a sad mouse in overalls and a red paisley shirt. Perhaps a miniature farm. The tiny fences, wooly trees, stubby oxen, and the red windmill fit into a six-inch-long steamer trunk. "No, that's too delicate. It would get smashed right away," Fred warned. "That's more like it—" pointing to a yellow plastic tank and a white motorcycle helmet. "Andy will want a gun."

The guns were very satisfactory; they grunted moodily and puffed acrid smoke. Fred bought all the children guns and a tank. So armed, they walked like partisans with weapons they were proud of having wrestled from the clerks.

The living room was a jungle of wrapping paper. The packages were white shrouds over turrets, triggers, barrels, and tank treads.

"I hate Christmas," Fred confessed. "It's worse every year. If they say they want a bike, some kid up the block gets a motorcycle. You lay out forty dollars on trains, and they tell you Christmas afternoon they really wanted a radio-controlled plane. You can never do the right thing by children, I guess."

He threw the last parcel under the tree and turned toward her a tired face on which misery had traced gray lines. She wanted to take him in her arms, but asked him instead to see whether the garage door was closed. Errands cheered him; he supposed if you could construct a life of enough distractions you could become immortal.

On Christmas Day, the living room looked like a departure station for a children's crusade. Everyone liked the guns enormously, even Hallie, who was given the chance to play general and refuse every request.

.   .   .

Although the winter may seem to be all holidays, between are stretches of ordinary days when the heat sings into the radiators, creaking and withering the house. There are dark nights with soft petals of snow under the street light's circle. On a few Saturdays and Sundays when there were storms, Lillian expected that they would eat pancakes and maple syrup and chew through a pile of old *Geographics*, but Fred spent an anxious window-watching half hour in the house, then bounded out to test the snow blower and to sprinkle steps with rock salt before the ice could form.

She called, "Your rubbers. Your scarf. You forgot your hat," not because they seemed necessary, but because she had heard Phyllis shout them. And Fred waved back carelessly, as he always had. He never stopped long enough to be told how much she wanted to belong to him.

She was thinking about that as she lay on the ground beside the car in which he had been crushed. They were on their way home, after the large meal they always ate on Thursdays at the Cathay Pagoda, when Fred braked the car suddenly and trees began to fly by the windows at absurd angles.

For two mornings after that, she taught herself what had happened. Otherwise, she might have confused the body in the box with so many—her mother, father, Phyllis. She was protected from silence and thought by masses of people who surrounded her in the living room, in the funeral home, at the church. Dignified by their responsibility, they treated the house deferentially, as if it were an extension of Fred. They were extremely polite to one another and touched frequently, assuring one another of their own life, each second losing the sense of uselessness and horror.

After the cemetery, she went upstairs to lie down, while Ben's wife served coffee and trays of heavy pastry: "You should have something in your stomach for the long ride." Afraid of hurting her and fearful of not showing respect, each held a great, sticky roll in one hand and a paper cup of steaming coffee in the other and wondered what to do with them.

The dead man's house was beginning to look like their own. His daughter had stopped crying and was taking aspirin at the kitchen sink; his grandchildren were laughing on the back porch. The cousins from Trenton, who were invaluable at wakes, were becoming tedious in attempts to prolong the tragedy by recalling Lillian's dazed face: "She doesn't *know* yet. When everyone's gone, she'll find something of his and break up over it. You saw how near the breaking point she was at the cemetery, didn't you?"

When they left, Lillian did try to possess the house, but she could not touch anything and call it hers. To whom do I belong now? she wondered. Father Morrissey stayed a safe distance away: once, in the Stop and Shop parking lot, tipping his black felt hat cautiously to her. Hallie said: "He asked me if you wanted him to call—he's exceptionally thoughtful, you know; but I told him that you'd let him know if you wanted any help." What kind of help he could bring was not certain. Lillian considered pictures of cardinals, bishops, the Pope in news magazines; she read articles about the Council; she was unmoved and only guilty because she had not felt deprived.

Things happened, she believed. Places were. People were. They slipped into a function from which they could scarcely vary; some waited quietly, taking only a little space like a tree or a stone, for the weather to fall on them. In the long run, they were the best off and caused the least damage. As for herself, her purpose had been to be on the edge, saving other people from whatever was on the other side, like a beach or the face of a mountain or the sawdust and crinkled newspaper in boxes around perishables. This is the way I am, she thought; things and people decide they need care, fall apart, become defenseless when I appear. It is in the nature of things that I am not very good even at taking care, but must. She worried so much that she fidgeted, lost, dropped, mislaid, spent afternoons in paralyzing black clouds of worry, and later could not remember what about. She stuck her head into rooms tentatively and often froze like a hunting dog in the middle of a step.

I must visit Fred and Phyllis, she thought, and left their house to drive to the gates of Precious Blood Cemetery, and then down the broad avenue, toward the great calvary group on the hill. The Ryans were on the third street off the avenue. A hundred years before the earliest Ryan arrival had bought a plot when the first Catholic staked out a few acres of sandy soil near the town dump as a burying ground. Now the cemetery had become the largest in the city, its early iron fence replaced by hedges. At first, off on the ragged edges, Polish and Italian babies lay in single lots; these were overtaken by flashy stones with engraved roses and sometimes an inlaid photograph. The oldest part of the cemetery had almost no new burials now; the little obelisks and pillars were covered with names and lichen, and few cars stopped there to release weeping women.

Fred had come out here once a week, but what he had done on his visits was not clear to Lillian. She had gone with her mother before Memorial Day to take geraniums to various graveyards. For a few minutes they dug energetically, settled in the geranium pot, looked pleased at the result. Then they got into the car, and returned the next Memorial Day. It was assumed that someone would steal the plant or rabbits would eat it or it would otherwise disappear. Catholics, Lillian observed, made a production of cemetery visits; unsatisfied with perpetual care, they brought lawn mowers and clippers, washed the monuments, pulled the crab grass and snipped the dandelions, and scowled at her sitting in the car. In the newer part, the activity was intense; families scrambled out of cars, fell kneeling on the grass in all weather, cried and stroked the fresh graves.

In there, she thought, they are lying—one would think there would be more to show for it. My grave would never be so tidy. It would wear signs of struggle. How can I lie here with these neat people?

With great sinking of heart, she realized that she had timed the visit badly and so had Father Morrissey, who was at the moment on one of his rare trips to see whether the sexton had been drinking on the job—not that the priest cared what he did, but irate cemetery visitors brought tales to the rectory. "He was making faces, Father, when he was clipping around Monica's headstone. He stole the K. of C. marker from Dad's grave, I'm sure. When he dug for little Joey, he tried to break into Cousin Ray's vault. I don't like to say this because everyone knows that alcoholism is a disease, but you can smell it after him. One day last summer, Father, I drove by Pat Killourey's monument, and he was sprawled out behind, his mouth wide open. I'm broad-minded, but a drunk in the cemetery . . ."

Another sexton could not be found, nor could the old

one be persuaded to find work elsewhere. Father Morrissey
hated trouble, and except for complaints about the sexton,
most of the flock protected him from their major miseries.
They admired his shiny car, his well-fed frame, his glittering
glasses, and his unlined face, and did not wish to chip away
any of the prosperity.

He swept briskly from behind a tree, and Lillian, realizing
that neither of them could hide, straightened her spine.

"Ah, visiting, Mrs. Ryan. Calm out here, isn't it?"

"Yes, it certainly is. You keep the cemetery in wonderful
condition."

"We try, we try, Mrs. Ryan. Same housekeeping problems
you have in your own home. Hard to get good help. Have to
keep on top of the work."

Talk stalled. Trying to jolt it free, they began together and
interrupted each other.

"I wonder . . ." she said.

"I suppose . . ." he said. "Go ahead, Mrs. Ryan. We all
wonder a lot. What do you wonder?"

She had been going to ask him if he thought she ought to
be buried out here, on the other side of Phyl, with Fred between them, but she decided to be more central.

"I wonder if I cared enough for Fred?" Father Morrissey
looked as if she had hit him. She hastened to explain herself.
"I mean, I might have kept him from being killed."

"How could you? It was God's will."

"Oh, no, you don't understand. I could have taken so much
better care of him."

"How?"

"I never seem to do anything right, or to do anything, for that matter. I have spent most of my life sitting around like a pigeon, waiting for things to happen."

"In the eternal design, one cannot be certain if one's action will be approved by God. How can man's finite eyes read His message?" Mrs. Ryan's eyes certainly did not. They settled on his dusty shoes without hope or color. Accustomed to this look, he launched into sermon style. "Each one of us has a responsibility to save our soul. One step at a time."

"It all seems so far away."

"What seems so far away, Mrs. Ryan?"

"Heaven, or whatever it is that happens afterward. Where they are now."

"Who, Mrs. Ryan?"

"Fred and Phyl—" turning her head toward the two markers.

"God's ways are very difficult. We're only human, you know." He did not look as if he believed it. Pastoral counseling under the trees and the airplanes was impossible. "I wish you'd come to see me at the rectory some afternoon. We could have a good talk about all this."

"Oh, I don't want to talk about it. All I want to know is, Father, how long am I supposed to stay married to Fred? How do you go about getting a divorce from the dead?"

Father Morrissey leaned against the monument. He fixed his eyes on a cluster of Norway spruce near the gates. The world is a mad place, he reminded himself, and loneliness causes insanity. He had always been disturbed by stories of hermits and of the desert fathers.

"The Church, as you know, disapproves of divorce. Anyway, I don't see what divorce has to do with you."

"It has everything to do with me. How can Fred be married to both of us? And now they're supposed to be somewhere together and I'm here in their house, opening the closet doors and seeing their clothes inside. And suppose there is some kind of afterlife: what are they going to do with me? Are we all going to sit on the front porch together and go out to dinner?"

"It's not like that, Mrs. Ryan."

"Well, I don't suppose anybody knows how it is. But one thing I am sure of, I can't stay married to him. It's not right."

Father Morrissey decided to hunt the sexton another time. The best way to deal with people who were not themselves, he believed, was to walk away as if nothing were wrong. Therefore, he backed off from Lillian cautiously, giving a little wave of dismissal. "Now you must try very hard not to be morbid. The next time we meet I want to see you more cheerful."

He wondered if he should wave again as he drove out of the cemetery, but decided to keep his eyes on the neat crushed-stone road.

THE HAPPIEST
YOU'VE
EVER BEEN

Lois was especially good with old people, unobtrusively putting a hand under their elbows on the steps, patching their mothy memories with hearty laughter. On Sundays, for instance, you would find her at safe relish-tray restaurants, chomping away on well-done chops at a table full of elderly women in jersey or crepe half-sizes, studying their faces, and smiling while she chewed deliberately. It is hard to chew and smile at the same time, but she managed gracefully. Another aspect of the picture of her that you might carry in your head was that she wore silver-framed glasses, but in truth she wore no glasses at all. That was the way your memory would be fooled with the pictures of Lois Sedway that you might manufacture. But not many people bothered.

Her appearing with old people was one way of staying young and gaining a great helping of virtue effortlessly, but the virtue-collecting was entirely unconscious. You would have thought that she was involved enough in good works during the week. Lois was a marriage counselor for a religious agency, and all her days listened to variations of despair caused by too little money, sex, youth, talk, or horror—or too much sex, youth, talk, or horror. Lois listened by not listening at all.

"Remember, Miss Sedway? Remember, I told you last week how he yells at me all the time?"

"What does he yell about?"

"Oh, you know. In the daytime the kids—they make too much noise. Or they don't make enough. They're pouring sand into gas tanks, eating plaster off the wall. And at night—"

They sat in a glassed-in cubicle. The client stared over the glass at the eighteen inches of open air between the top of the glass and the ceiling.

"Yes," Lois asked. "At night, what?"

The client avoided her eyes. She had rehearsed this part of the story several times that morning and on the bus and had enjoyed his mountainous gall—what he had wanted in bed after he called her every name and had thrown all the ravioli across the room onto the café curtains. But now she looked past the glass partition and her dry throat could not relate one syllable of her insults in bed. The planned speech faded like a gritty snowman. She was ashamed of herself for dwelling on those dark doings in the tired sheets and especially in the presence of this lady in navy blue with the white collar attached by a gold pin with an urn and birds flying over it that was too ugly not to be an antique and valuable.

"In bed it's not very good either," she ventured and bowed her head.

That is why Lois Sedway was such a successful marriage counselor. No one told her anything. Many problems solved themselves: alcoholics drank themselves into hospitals, wives who had been beaten every night discovered they could work the night shift and have a pay check too, children who could not learn to read left school and became truck drivers, remembering the routes by landmarks and avoiding danger by the shape of the road signs. People healed themselves while Lois waited, caring but not listening, her reputation for goodness being magnified.

Stability was treasured as a rare coin in her office. Everything there moved in double time; clients zoomed past like water bugs; the shape of their stories glittered with temporarily fascinating variations; caseworkers fled to graduate school or real estate selling. "Would you take my African violets and this old blotter and, oh Lois, why don't you move into my office? It has two windows."

She not only got the plants, the office with two windows, and the hard-core descendants of hard-core problem cases, but seniority for vacation choice, which she spent at one mountain lodge or another with much older women who had mislaid or lost their husbands or mothers. Between meals they rocked on the porches or sifted through jetsam in antique shops, looking for objects the owner was guaranteed not to have. Lois had occasional opportunities for marriage, none for love. The last time an offer was presented by a caseworker who smelled of wax paper and used a nose inhaler. Stroking his receding gums, he sat bunched up in the driver's seat.

They were parked outside her apartment; he folded his legs and staring at her with fearful sacrifice asked: "Are you in perfect health? I have to be sure of that." Until that question, she had been resigned to the marriage proposal.

Surrounded daily by the ruins of other people's dreams, Lois suspected they would have been a lot happier not looking for happiness at all. From a great distance she studied those labeled successes and those called failures and decided that they were about the same height. As events and people eroded in the burning gaze of time and habit, none of the things that were announced to matter mattered at all. What difference did it finally make what you wore or whom you married or whether you had children or whether you didn't. Yet the clients staked all upon these magic expectations. For these they gambled, raped, stole, beat their children, and tried suicide.

Lois Sedway had deliberately lost her identity; to herself she was anyone and no one. "You have," a long-ago roommate had said one loose-mouthed midnight when generalizations came easy, "you have a man's mind. It studies out people and things, but never really attaches itself." The roommate had been right. Helmeted within the wavy cap of hair was a head that had grown so dispassionate that it no longer belonged to one person. Each day on waking, Lois found herself slower to resume her identity, such as it was.

Paradoxes played in her head. Her brain was much of the time buzzing, chasing itself along cool boulevards or crooked lanes, moving her into other people's lives and back again. Listening to music or cutting up vegetables or waiting for sleep, she was thinking about the clients. Marjorie Delman, engaged but unmarried, five illegitimate children, perfumed and smiling as she awaited the perfect gentleman with hat and vest, who would open car doors for her. She had cut a photograph of Dr. Kildare from the *TV Guide* and tacked it to the closet door. "The kind of man I want for my babies' father, Miss Sedway." Some of Lois also crawled into the skull of thin Michael Napoli, who bit off two of his kid sister's toes before throwing her onto the porch roof. In the unadoptable children's center he pulled apart all the furniture and gouged the walls until they kept him in a bare green cell. "I always read that Dr. Spock book you gave me," Mrs. Napoli complained, "but it didn't make no difference with him. He was what you might call unique, wasn't he?"

The ugliest people in her case load were the poorest and those stuck in the largest tangle of misfortune. Her poor had limp hair, thin teeth, poor posture, spotty skin, bad breath, wretched handwriting. Compensations? She had yet to find them. The richest girls at college, the ones with raised coats of arms on their stationery, so rich they never carried money, like royalty—they had copped the good teeth and the curly hair. They had married the good-looking if nondescript men, and their handwriting was impressive and their children's chins were firm enough to outlast any disasters. Lois searched for a commendable feature or two in each face in the shambling line. For the first few months of the job she had mentally rebuilt lives at random, gifting a phantom or two with clear skin and neat waist, but after a few years these ceased to be norms, and she wondered why they had ever seemed desirable.

There is more than one way to be blind, stupid, lonely, lazy, and dirty, Lois knew. Her clients were only wicked in the most obvious manner. Lois in her white collar and cuffs brushing dandruff from her navy-blue shoulder could be wicked in far more exotic dimensions than they would have known possible. Her case loads had reached the ridiculous point that she failed to connect names and problems, but none of that made any difference. She wondered what made her stay. Goodness? A neurotic sense of superiority? Habit? Indolence? All these, none and more. A weather vane of possible lives for herself whirred in her head. That cycles of guilt, terror, boredom, hatred, and love played in her head never showed on the broad undisturbed planes of her face. And she did not join the Peace Corps or become a broker or go back to Indiana. Nothing I do could possibly harm the clients, she thought. But can anything I do make life better for them?

When she began asking this question hourly, she searched out some of her old college friends sleeping deeper into middle age, whose lives she wanted to compare with her own. It was difficult to talk with them through the net of interruptions strung around their houses, rushing boys and dogs, circling trays of cheese balls and herring on toothpicks, and a powerhouse of appliances working or not working— blenders, mixers, choppers, washers, driers. She crawled from the arenas with a few general impressions.

In college she had been a parlor liberal, worn a Stevenson button, marched in a rally or two. But some of these girls had spoken at ADA meetings, petitioned for McCarthy's censure, announced themselves for free love, stormed the offices of trustees who had fired a card-carrying math profes-

sor, had become math majors and crowded into his dull advanced classes and threatened to leave college if he were not
kept on. Lois wondered where all their bravery had gone.

They now sat in middle-priced housing units deep in noisy,
tumbling kids, distracted from complete sentences by mop-
ping messes and shoving cereal, seeking Sunday's hour of
peace while good silent graying Mac or Bob or Stan took over
guard duties in the living room. They had become Sunday
church-goers. "Liberal? You've no idea how free-spirited our
congregation is. We had a swarmi last week and we've had
rabbis and Rosicrucians and Bahais and a Little Sister of the
Poor." Then they would tell Lois about the yogi exercise
group and their Negro minister in such a way that it was
obvious she should praise them.

Her own liberalism yawned like an abyss. If the process of
leveling continued, she would wind up as a client—or like
Max Bodenheim or Joe Gould. There were days when
she studied approaches to normalcy. That was like salting
a bird's tail; just when you thought you were close enough to
capture normalcy, it took off in an unexpected direction.

Some of the most dedicated rebels exist among us like spies,
their external lives monuments of incredible ordinariness.
When she looked back at her childhood, Lois saw there only
great portents of commonness, as if she had been selected
to illustrate some statistically average American. What she
remembered of home were fields greening into winter wheat,
the smell of an alfalfa mill, a grove of willows beside
the muddy river, mourning doves throbbing on the telephone
wires, and a fresh breeze sliding over the farm in early May

that proved they had survived the winter. It was also the
windmill clacking through windy nights and sooty lamp
shades before the electric wires reached to her father's farm,
fluted nostrils of great swaying shorthorns as they drank deep
from the mossy wooden tough, and clouds of dust chasing
the Plymouth along the ditches, the dark steamy cold of the
snowed-in barn and for several months mud everywhere—in
the entry at school, in chunks on the flowered stair carpet, or
clotted on the cows' bellies. Her red-cheeked brothers filled
the silos; her silent mother did the dishes, staring out the
kitchen window at her barred Rocks; on Saturdays they sat
on backless benches watching bronco busters in the dusty
rodeo ring. Children there seemed to grow into sturdy and
sensible farm agents, tractor salesmen, or Lutheran ministers, or at least those that stayed. But some great insecurity
probably ate their solid flesh and sure minds. More than all
discoveries Lois treasured the one that guaranteed the basic
similarity of flesh under skin and the way death crouches in
the same corner of everyone's skull.

   This knowledge propelled her to fall happily and permanently in love with Art DelGardo. Art DelGardo had a wife,
five grown kids, twenty-two apartment houses—the basement
of one of them full of lottery slips—a roofing company, and a
face shaped for smiling. He liked the way he lived well enough
to stuff his wallet with a lot of credit cards and his body with
a lot of vitamins to make sure that he wouldn't stop. In his
fifty-fifth year he tucked in his belly and parted his hair
further back. Mame DelGardo had her own car, and he guessed
spent her days carting the grandchildren from shopping centers to factory outlets to cut-rate drug stores. She was so busy

grabbing bargains that she bought twice what everybody could use and packed the rest off to unknown relatives in the Azores who sent back pictures of themselves wearing all the factory outlet garments, sagging on their skinny frames and no shoes on their spread-out feet. The Old Country—he had been born there and thought of it only as the smell of eucalyptus and the sun drying out his bones down to the yellow marrow. The Old Country was unwashed sweat and sour milk and cheap olive oil.

Anyway, Art DelGardo rode his silver Lincoln from tenement to tenement, staring into plugged drains and frowning at garbage-strewn basements. When they asked for screens, his mouth dropped in astonishment. "You want I should go bankrupt? Not for that I came from Fayal with one pair of pants, that you should bust screens in my own house. You want screens? You make them out of the web of the spider?" They gave up needing screens in favor of new bathtubs flat on the floor.

"Want, want, all the time. The eyes from this head. What you want is for me to go bankrupt. You suck my bones."

He kept no account books. Only little pieces of paper ripped from a looseleaf book and folded into pockets behind the monogrammed handkerchiefs. He never had to look at them again. No one knew, and when Mame DelGardo asked him what she should do if he got sick, he asked her what she had a guardian angel for anyway.

The accountant hired yearly because someone had said he was good at tax dodges shrank into pasty-faced despair. "No receipts, no checks, Art. How can we get deductions, if we don't have figures?"

"Make up some. Pick a number. Square ones. Round ones. Dream a number."

Art would have liked to be a kidder, but no explorer had excavated this hope. In his mind, roomfuls of roaring strangers punched his ribs and scooped handfuls of tears from their faces in the tide of his funniness. He longed to wear a camel's-hair coat and a white broad-brimmed hat, but store windows and the bathroom mirror told him he was a neat little lump of a man with a half hour's worth of mucus in his morning throat. His real talent would be discovered by Lois Sedway.

None of his family knew about the apartment houses— how many there were, where, and who lived in them. He shopped for new ones with particular notions about lucky days, Tuesdays, for instance. He often began projects on Tuesdays—would pass a large house that needed fixing and walk carefully through the basement, feeling the underpinning, estimating the termites per square foot. On the whole he was accurate about both termites and underpinning. He could see the domestic miracles possible in cut-away drawings in his head. First, a pock-marked house slumped into marsh or squatted in a weedy sandpit. A few days after Art DelGardo passed his hands over the underpinning, a new roof covered the place, thick petunias fell out of windowboxes, and the rents had jumped a hundred per cent. In his head Art moved all the houses onto one street, so that they stretched beyond the limits that one person could see. Let Mame DelGardo wear out her knees in church; these houses were his redemption.

Only genuine disaster drove Lois from her office. Over the telephone Mrs. Diolis had threatened to put her head in the oven after she had poured Draino over the children's cereal. Then she had slammed down the receiver of the pay phone. By the time Lois had reached the apartment house, everything the Diolises owned in part or whole was piled onto a dump truck: the chairs with sprung seats, a nest of stained mattresses, bent pots and pans, a hamster squashed in one corner of a littered cage. It was both more and less than she had thought the Diolises owned. A tangle of children were in the cab of the truck and Mrs. Diolis leaned against it, scratching her forearms. She had certain predictable gestures; when she waited for answers, she scratched her arms. Lois nodded to give assurance. "What you must do, Mrs. Diolis, is wait for me to find the landlord. Wait here."

"Where would I go anyway?"

Upstairs, Lois found Art DelGardo looking into closets. He chewed his lower lip when she asked: "Why can't you take fifty dollars and put them back?"

"Why?" He looked straight into her face.

"Because you don't have another tenant."

"Eight rooms, good heat, lots of light, near everything— and no one's going to take it? You got your head screwed on wrong."

She felt that perhaps she might. "It's got rats and drafts and roaches and smells like someone's dead. You'll wait five years before anybody'll take it off your hands." The brassiness of her voice banged around the room.

Art DelGardo put thumbs into his suit pockets and cocked

his head. He seemed absorbed in smelling exactly how dead someone might be or guessing whether the closet might become a lavette.

She arranged another attack. "Think how happy Mrs. Diolis would be to return to her home."

"It's not her home. I pay the taxes and fix the drains. She doesn't even have a lease."

"You should be ashamed. Everyone deserves that security."

"Why? No one ever gave it to me just because they liked my face."

"Look at them," Lois pointed out a smudged pane at the family lounging below.

"A mess," he said at her shoulder. "Why should I spill tears on that. Let them dig holes in somebody else's plaster." Looking at her bright wind-blown hair he remembered that Mame DelGardo had a head like a stone woman he had seen years ago in a Lisbon museum, every massive curl and wave indestructible.

"Women," he said. "They wreck you every time. They'd push you over the cliff for the insurance. Like you. Do you care one eye blink for that wagon load down there? So, it's your job. But care? Squeeze your heart ten minutes for them? Talk straight across, eyes to eyes the way we're doing now? I guess not."

"You're not supposed to get involved with individual cases. But I care because I might be down there evicted on the street and you might too."

"Maybe you. Not me. For you I give up. Let's pretend we're smarter than we are and go talk about this somewhere over coffee. I can't think right without coffee."

So the Diolis family spread their goods in the same pattern as before, and Art and Lois sat in a shiny cafeteria among the sliding trays and used-up people, and whatever it was began between them, not romance or affair, simply eating often and sleeping occasionally together, but not really together. "I like you," he said that day in the cafeteria. "You fight clean. Like a man. And you don't talk like you knew everything. That's good."

Ten years before, she would have wondered what they had to give and gain. She might have been annoyed by his shaking hand, his dactylic cough, by his running his lower lip under his teeth in a quick sweep. A year later if some stranger had described these traits she would have denied their existence. The inexplicable fact was that she fell in love as people do in fables or even more like those who have passions that no one else can comprehend—for dangerous mountains, for unpleasant animals like crocodiles, for the smell of tar, for silence itself. The external results were imperceptible; afraid to betray her speeding blood, she moved even more slowly at work. But within herself she began tearing down walls she had built and throwing the pieces at herself so that she could hear the destruction of her old self. What she tried to do in the agency was to bring her clients to her degree of freedom by solving the problems in the foreground. When you're free, you don't think about it. She tried to give this freedom to the clients, and she tried not to cut down Art DelGardo's enormous supply. For one thing, they never fought. The first time they had slept together, he had warned her not to talk a great deal and not to expect a great deal. She did neither, and consequently, never communicated the miracle she found there.

Wrapped in a kind of cellophane, they stirred faintly just out of touch. Since they met at night, the silver Lincoln assumed, depending upon their moods, the dimensions of public and private place. It was house, airplane, apartment, or park bench. It tunneled beneath black tree shapes fall and winter and whispered grandly along turnpikes in the green months toward beaches along which they walked sturdily. Sometimes they parked on a dry promontory overlooking the city—a sprawling yellow river and great oil tanks beyond which gulls rode. Art DelGardo was very fond of birds: under his very white shirt a silver Holy Ghost hung against his dark spongy chest. When they had eaten, rapidly, what they wanted of a large pizza, he tore the cold wedges into smaller pieces and threw them toward the gulls. But the birds were too old or stubborn to flatter and waited until he got back into the car before they swooped down. He smiled at them through the windshield. "That's what I like about animals. They take. You don't give them anything. No gifts, no obligations. That's being free. That's more than you can say for all those wrecks that come in to see you. Tell me, what help can you really give them?"

"Try to keep them moving, patch them up, that's all. Just try to keep down some new kind of decay that's threatening."

"I don't get it, never have. A man has to scramble up the sides of the pit himself. My troubles, God knows, I've had them."

"What troubles? What troubles did you have?"

"Why should I tell you? Even if you'd been there, what good would that have done? Troubles? When a man hides from trouble, he's dead. Thirty years ago I had a mortgage note on my car, a sick mother, three babies, and one good shirt, and I put the good shirt on and went out and bought a house. A farmer named Isaac Bingell gave me the money at seven per cent and my mother got sicker and I lost my job at the lace mill, but I fixed that house over. Oh, what do you care about it?"

"You were healthy. Everybody isn't as strong as you were."

"I made myself strong. As a kid I learned fast, how to sign my report card and lie to make sure my mother was out of the house when the homeroom teacher came on a visit to find out how many beds and whether we had an inside toilet and an electric range. See, even then, somebody was watching what we did and trying to make us weak. They never got us down in any book. We were always too smart."

"What does all that prove?"

"It proves that we didn't need anybody to pull us along, that's what. It proves I wasn't a runny-nosed kid crying to Mama all the time. I made it myself, see."

There was no point in answering. He was active every second, even sleeping or sitting, not twitching or fingering, but every cell of him was purposely devoted to that moment.

One night they were walking past a skating rink sprinkled with tight-bodied children all miraculously swooping and swirling without falling. It was neither too cold nor damp nor too early or late, and that much of Lois Sedway had never been in one place before, able to hear or understand what was immediately before her and what might at that second be happening in a back alley in Salerno or a village without a name on the Amazon or anywhere in the world.

"Tell me," he asked her. "When in your life were you happiest? When in your whole life?"

She had wanted to shout that it was at this exact second before they could walk one step further, but she only said: "I don't know. How can you know what was the happiest until they are all finished and one rises above all the others like a mountain over the plain? Do you know when you were happiest?"

"Oh, yes. That skating rink made me think of it. The day my son was born. I could not think of anything but the fact that I had made him. A man. To make a man is a wonderful thing. I never forgot the feeling. He didn't work out the way I hoped, but I never held that against him. What mattered was that morning and the way I felt."

They watched the spectacular toys twisting, swishing, turning, waving at parents, sweeping toward danger, banking, gliding. Lois told him he would get a chill and should get back into the car, which they did.

·   ·   ·

Four months later Mame DelGardo awakened one spring morning to a heavy silence, and looking across the gray room, knew before she ran to touch him that Art DelGardo's heart had stiffened and stopped before he could cry out.

THE

COLLECTION

Every single time I come home, the same conversation begins all over again. It starts, actually, the minute my mother has parked in two spaces in front of the terminal and I climb into her oversized Cadillac. I play this particular game of conversation so well that I am not there at all but operating on automatic control entirely. You know, the way you learn a particular road until your car automatically brakes before the potholes it knows about, so you're half asleep and find yourself in the garage unconscious of the last hour and the car without a scratch so it must have been all right.

I'm certainly not a great thinker about my childhood except when I come home about once a year to this town where there is no present, only past, for me. It probably doesn't have any future for anybody that stayed there. If fate had poured glue over my shoes, I would be sitting in a cozy knotty-pine den watching the five o'clock movie on TV while my lovely childhood sweetheart Dido Cyr, now turned into a grumpy middle-weight, would be shoving a frozen chicken pot pie into the oven, and our messy kids would be trampling the eight or nine blades of grass left in the back yard.

While my mother aims the car homeward, she casts over

our heads the tangled history of the last year in the slight joys and big miseries of faintly recognizable children I knew thirty years ago who are now wandering the middle-aged desert. My home town could be a museum for the Northeastern mill village, full of three-deckers shingled with fake brick and rancid little grocery stores. Everything in it from the porch swings to the glass ashtrays in the shape of top hats came right out of the 1939 edition of the Sears, Roebuck catalog except for the forests of extended TV antennas. Typically, reception is poor in our valley.

At some mysterious point in her narrative, my mother, that master of indirection, introduces her grand design for my future.

"I'd be tickled to death," she always says, "tickled to death, if you'd join us."

She is talking about my coming home forever, joining the firm. We are and have been death merchants. Why weasel out of it and call us benefactors? Somebody has to do it. We happen to be embalmers and funeral directors. You may have seen the sign, A. Maigrey and Sons. Not really a family business any more. The first Alphonse, the one on the sign, he with the wing collar and cutaway in the office photo, was my great-grandfather. Now there is only my older brother, also an Alphonse, God help him, and what is left of my father, a quivering mass of nerves, shrunk in the middle, big in the ears and feet, the way the old get. Out in the back, beyond the showroom, sits the hired assistant, often a new one, too poor or scared to go out on his own, studying for a license, mealy-mouthed to Alphonse's face, behind his back gossiping about his drinking and our cheapness.

Anyway, the business has always been a fact of life with me. We used to live over the caskets and embalming rooms, but in those days everyone was waked at home, whether in a tenement or out on a farm.

So in this particular conversation with my mother last spring she announced the usual invitation: "If you came home, you could take over the office and Alphonse could do what he was trained to do. I never liked this assistant, and your father, he's no good for anything since the stroke."

"You forget that I have a job."

"What business is it to fly? A life, you call it, flying over people's back yards like a bird? A life out of suitcases in hotels? Some day leaving your children orphans, not remembering what you looked like?"

You notice that my mother does not mention my wife. In this game of talk Eve does not exist. After my cremation in the suburb or the marsh, wherever I crash, the children will be certified public orphans. For a moment I saw them in a faded procession of other orphans in smocks, two by two, along a dusty road, led and followed by puffing nuns. They would be successful orphans. I dismissed the procession sure that my orphans can lie, steal, and cheat well. Secure in that, I put down my strongest card.

"The pay is better than I could get doing anything else. What do I know how to do?"

"Don't be so stuck up about the business. Last winter we sent about ten cases over to the Massés' we were so busy here."

"You sent cases away?" I didn't have to pretend to be shocked. All women are materialists, but sometimes they can or want to disguise it. My mother never bothers to cover it up. Her name isn't on the license, but she knows more about linings for the boxes and how to place the hands and what flowers hold their shape in a hot parlor than Alphonse or the assistant could learn in a fifteen-year apprenticeship to a Fifth Avenue chapel. She has run every rival director to the ground in a maximum of five years' competition. And always remained friendly enough with them at the end to buy out all their supplies. She is especially fond of kneeling benches and background drapes in the same rich mulberry velvet.

She's a wise collector. There's nothing malicious about it. She just happens into houses when customers are getting ready to leave fifty or sixty years' of carved sideboards, worn carpets, and shabby kitchen tables. Sometimes a daguerreotype or an old-fashioned cameo is lying inside one of the drawers. A lot of the families at the unloading stage have no young connections, so Mother becomes their best friend for a few months. She drives them out to the grave and then back into town, stopping at the Dairy Queen for a cone, and they visit back and forth. They need someone to help them over a bad time, and the things they give Mother are really pay for a service. She's picked up some very nice furniture and jewelry that way.

"So it was a good year?" I asked.

"We could have had three in here at one time," she said. "If we'd had the room, but you build on and what happens

—only singles for a couple of years. I'd rather have the steady hundred a month from the people renting upstairs, unless you surprise us and come home, and then we'd get more business, and have another chapel up there."

I saw the house in a kind of cutaway drawing, each of the three chapels, the good, better, best in use, their green metal chairs filled by decent, heavy mourners.

"It's Alphonse that brings the business, not me."

"Alphonse came too late."

She's right. If ever a man was born into the wrong time, it's my brother, Alphonse. I used to think it was a stage he would outgrow or a bad gimmick that he'd learn to throw away, but he's never shown any other side of himself so I guess we're stuck with the Alphonse they sent us. He licks his lips all the time, and he likes dressing up in morning clothes. On him they look good. He had a paunch in the third grade. He belongs to the Legion and the 40 & 8 and the Marquette Alliance.

Every other undertaker I've ever seen sits outside the church in the cab of the hearse, smoking or reading the paper until it's time to come in for the body. But not Alphonse. He stands at the rear of the church, legs apart, hands clasped in front, checking on the general respectability. He's a great toucher, too, pressing arms and backs in vague sympathy, and if he knows the client at all, he has been seen crying at the cemetery. People really hate this. Death is a private business, and strangers horning in like Alphonse annoy the hell out of them. About thirty years ago, he would have been perfect. If what is left of a family is over fifty, they like Alphonse, but I've seen young women pull themselves away as he tried to hold them by the arm when they were selecting a box in the showroom. They didn't want their backs stroked; they wanted to know the total price (we keep that on a card hanging from the rear hinge). What people really care about is how to probate the will and how to make over the joint account.

"I wrote you about Norman Bothwick, didn't I?" my mother asked. "He had it in both lungs. Skin and bones, that's all. Drink did it. It was during the cold spell in January. Couldn't bury him for more than a month. Finally they had to dynamite. It was frozen down to seven feet."

"How is Dido?" I asked.

"Well, she hasn't paid yet, isn't likely to. Drunk all the time. Alphonse will have to go down sometime this week."

"You'd better let me," I said. "That's one thing I can do. Is it for much?"

"Five hundred. That's with the mausoleum rent and the digging. It was only a gray cloth box."

"Look, I'll go this afternoon," I said. There are few excuses for leaving the house, and all of them have to do with money —taking it to the bank, getting more of it from somebody else.

The dream girl of my sullen adolescence, Dido Cyr, had married Norman Bothwick, now resting in his unpaid-for gray cloth covers. As a young girl, Dido had a starved look; her clothes seemed to have been bought for someone larger and she panted a little as if she had run a great distance or she couldn't find enough air. She had an expensive appetite, but she kept growing thinner until I thought I could see the ivory bones under her freckled arms. That kind of woman always blows up after fifty but continues to have the voice of a sparrow.

I can remember how hungry Dido Cyr's body looked from any angle because in our slow growing-up we had few distractions. A limited group of human beings were studied inch by inch until they became extensions of our own bodies. My childhood was in slow motion. I was waiting for something that never happened. Doing this, I sat on curbs a lot or leaned against walls, wearing out my corduroy knickers. My own children are greater realists; they do not wait agonizingly for a circus or the dim expectation of a stunt flyer who might somersault over the house as he did once four years ago. One flat comment is that we had a great deal of time to fill and waiting can eat up a lot of time. Also, we had a lot to look forward to. It was a rather brown time, and the Depression made us, although we didn't know it, pretty faded; our clothes had been washed too often. I'm always shocked at how Technicolor children are now.

There's a kind of certainty in brownness. You know you may go somewhere up out of it. In my first grade and all through the smelly rooms of every increasing grade was, among others, Dido Cyr. I suppose you think that's a made-up name, but I swear that it was and is true. In my town as children we could have mustered classical armies from our names: little Achille Geroux, Arcide LeBlanc, Hector Morency, Ulysse Belgrade. Dido Cyr had a brother Euclide, a year younger. In those days they were Ste. Cyr, of course, before our names began shedding excess syllables.

Dido Cyr, now Bothwick, became my frequent partner in

our miserable childhood fantasies. In those days we were crazy about messages suitable for autograph books that foretold what combinations we would marry in and how many children we would hatch at once. Those prophecies were as good preparation as any for growing old. Playing slot machines would have had the same effect. Up comes a symbol for you and locks into place, waiting to be matched, but past slide the other combinations. You are ready, they aren't. Or is it the other way around? Dido believed in novenas, miracles, and movie magazines. Her fluttering little fingers sparkled with dime-store rings. She probably believed absolutely that I would replace every splinter of glass with rubies and emeralds. Her scarecrow body leaned against me on our dull pilgrimages to the movies and Moreau's Spa. She was more silently devoted than any dog, but I could feel habit rusting me into some damp corner of that used-up town.

The army rescued me. Dido sent me heavy daily messages that told me nothing worth reading in all the pages. I wrote her the same letters I sent everybody else who had a claim on me—exactly the same. I would write out what looked like a good letter from any viewpoint and copy it over with a different opening and closing as many times as I had people to write. The army seemed to be waiting to use me too. They couldn't make up their mind whether I should kill men by jumping suddenly on them or skiing circles around them. They trained me in all the ways of killing but never gave me the chance. And then it was over, and they sent me with all my cleverness home.

In '47 you might have thought I'd have used the GI Bill

at U. Conn. I almost did. That's where Squirt Jarvis and Gerry Morin went, and we drove over to Storrs to register together in the fall of '47. Funny thing, I decided not to stay even before I got there. It was going through Willimantic, exactly going under the railroad bridge, that changed my mind. I suppose there are a lot of uglier places—Dubuque, maybe. Eve says I've got rotten taste in cities. Brussels, for instance, I loathe, and Amsterdam. That day on the way to Storrs I decided Willimantic looked sat-on or it had some kind of disease that could be contagious. So I called my father from the telephone booth outside the quonset which the three of us were supposed to share with eight other guys.

It's an infuriating human habit we all have to pick the one day that changed our destiny, but anything that cuts through the maze of crazy decisions and reduces our big bundle of guilts to one main one is all right with me. So I prefer to pin the whole blame of my immediate past—the last twenty years of it—on the way the light struck Willimantic as we drove out from under the railroad bridge. The mud could have helped too. That phone booth was set in a kind of valley that should have been left to the frogs and skunk cabbage— but no, bulldozers were shaking and whining by, churning up the mud to set in another row of cinder-block dormitories. So I stood in that booth in my clean chinos telling Father that I wasn't ready to settle down, persuading my mother that I wouldn't stay away another two years. Our voices minced across the wire, cautiously, like tightrope walkers, caught each other, and exchanged confidence.

"Dido Cyr has gone to college too. She's somewhere up there," my mother said tentatively.

"That's good," I said. "When I come back, I'll look her up."

But I didn't come back. Instead I told both of them to take care, hung up, and turned the Dodge north. I drove up through the Connecticut Valley, where the trees were stunned into brilliance and at night wild geese slid by me in the opposite direction. Now, I've done a lot of traveling since then, God knows, and to a lot of places that you're supposed to remember until you're cold, like Istanbul and Kashmir. But that fall was more real than any of them.

I got to Dartmouth on a Saturday afternoon and saw a whole fraternity house full of nuts with their dates, long-haired blondes—you remember, Veronica Lake style—all playing softball on the front lawn, but with oranges. So I helped them field what was left of crushed skins and pulp, until the whole yard and all of us smelled like the second shift in a Sunkist factory. The other days, I stopped in serious green-and-white towns with wide streets where overtidy women were already burning leaves. They were shutting thousands of blinds on the old summer hotels and rolling up the straw carpets from the sagging verandas through every mountain resort.

I suppose I was drunk with freedom—not much else—certainly not the three or four glasses of beer in the afternoons. At night I stayed in cabins and ate big dinners in imitation lodges with a lot of hunters from Boston, little insurance men who'd bought their own deer to take home. We talked at night loudly across the booths in the lodges, talk that I suppose all men are pleased at doing well—about dirty carburetors and spark plugs and shells and the fastest routes back to the city. But I wasn't going back. The road north got narrower, and finally across the Canadian border it was gravel spread with some kind of oil to keep down the dust. At Ste. Simone there was a big agricultural fair, and I went through the cattle sheds and the fancywork shows and watched the horses, those with thick, hairy legs pulling a ton of stones a few inches after their owners got down on their knees and implored every saint in the book and then whispered like lovers, pressing their lips against the horses' ears.

Years later I found out what I was doing that fall. The people I spend most of the time on the ground with now, Eve's family, are rich in explaining the conduct of every other human being at any given time. They are not good about themselves, but they have come to know my past better than I do. According to Eve's mother, whose heavy voice begins explanations of me with *"Exactement!"* and a flood of quick clauses to show that she has studied my case well, I was in the fall of '47 finding my past. She has made an elaborate psychological study of my pushing into the heavy green forest through which my people had plunged in the opposite direction about a hundred years before. I now defying the natural seasonal instinct. Even the geese knew better. The plain fact of the whole excursion is that I am curious and, anyway, I always take the longest distance between two points in flying, if they let me, and in talking, as you can see well now.

My parents had never insisted that I was Franco-American, nor made me speak French around the house, nor thought of sending me to a school like Mount St. André where from

morning café au lait until lights out you might as well have
been in Lyons as Holyoke, Massachusetts. My going up to Quebec that September had a lot of late adolescent nostalgia
about it, a sort of show-offy mixture of happiness to be free
after the army and sorrow that I hadn't been killed and that
I was in danger of being sucked into the mud of some no-
account town.

Barreling through small towns in Quebec, I was a stranger,
free of acting a son or brother. To the twentieth or so removed
cousins I was more obliging and gentler than I had ever dared
to be to anyone. One of them, Omar LeBoef, persisted in
calling me "Le Clown." So amid the fourteen stolid, white-
faced LeBoefs I was the big American clown.

You know how those Canadian farms looked then, great
cleared squares sown with oats and winter wheat, barns like
cathedrals with shining roofs, solid haystacks against the
blizzards, and the house, a nothing, just a big kitchen with a
black stove, diapers hanging always behind it. On one wall
terrible oleographs of the Pope and the king and the statue
of Ste. Anne de Beaupre; on the other livestock calendars. In
the center of the big linoleum-covered table the catsup, horseradish, mustard, and relish waited forever. All the rest of the
house was bedrooms, the boys upstairs, the girls down, and
Omar and Marie next to the kitchen. The whole place smelled
all the time of frying grease, even when the kitchen door
swung open for a lazy gust of wind on which a few hundred
flies rode in.

You wouldn't believe this, but I liked it, knowing, of
course, that the LeBoefs wanted something else out of me

than I wanted from them. But that's basic supply and de-
mand. I've never found it different in any friendship. This
time they wanted a life-size American clown to show off in
the village who could sing hot popular songs and knew all
about the movie stars. And like somebody reading an out-of-
date guide book, I was looking for *voyageurs* and Marie Chap-
delaine, which meant I had to look mighty hard or shut my
eyes to the real place. Anyway, I didn't disappoint them. They
used me; the whole lot of them, three layers deep, drove to
Mass in the Dodge instead of walking across the lots, and
we did a lot of dancing to Omar's fiddle and the accordion
one of the sons played.

Some times in your life for no reason at all you are healthier
for about a year or so. You see clearly and hear better. Your
hair shines and your nails don't break off. If you were an animal, you would grow a beautiful, expensive coat. Even your
brain is in better condition, and you know that you are on
the threshold of being able to explain your clairvoyance to
yourself and everybody else, but the gift is gone as it came.
That was a healthy time for me, and I remember having the
good sense to know that it was. I crossed the St. Lawrence
on the ferry at Levis, when October was blowing over the
Plains of Abraham and the Chateau, and I was terribly impressed.

If it had been a bad time for me, I would have spent my
day or so, gotten tired of playing historical figures, and gone
home. Eventually that way, I would have married Dido Cyr,
not directly, but with the necessary stalling, some hot strug-
gles on the back seat of the Dodge every Saturday night, and

a couple of nasty fights for the making-up later. But I was swept along on this windy healthiness. I finally wound up at the University in Montreal, but most of the time I was learning to fly. You see, that's how good I felt. I was also learning that François Mauriac was not the only Frenchman writing novels. The girl who taught me that was Eve, of course. Her father had died in the Resistance in Paris, and her mother came to Montreal to run a kind of boarding house. I had never seen anything like Eve's room. Things hung or leaned on the walls: masks, mantillas, posters, shawls. The light was vague, and we all sat on the floor or danced in our stocking feet. I only saw the room once in the daylight, and sometimes I think I never have seen Eve at all in any light, but we do have four children and live in Westmount in a Tudor house, all gables and stucco.

Between the then of my going up there and now were the trips home. At the beginning I felt that my mother was running briefing sessions for me so that I wouldn't have missed anything when it came time to get serious and come home. For the first few years everybody I knew was getting married and between those weddings I went to and those my mother described, I saw them all safely matched and mated in combinations I had not dreamed of. There was even someone left for my brother Alphonse, a thick-necked girl who inspired only one description, "sensible."

Obviously, for Dido Cyr there was Norman Bothwick, the one now resting in his unpaid-for gray cloth covers. Since I have taken you this far, I might run through the Bothwick family tree, except that it's twisted and broken off by a lot of recent storms. Anyway, according to the tree metaphor, Norman's branch was not sturdy, but sort of out of sight, covered over and protected by the other Bothwicks you might think of first. If you played with spools of thread as a child, you know that their name sat quietly on the paper label in the center of the spool. So, if you were in my town, one Bothwick was almost as good as the next. Except that you can put your money on the wrong horse with a dandy name.

"He begins things," my mother said of Norman. "He's good at starts. Like the last census. He got all the thick books and pencils from the central office in Hartford and got dressed up to take an indoctrination course. But when he had to go into the first house, he didn't want to ask them about bathrooms and all that, and he just said he'd come back the next day and went out and threw away all the books behind a hedge and pretended he didn't know what happened to them."

Statistically, when Norman became a figure himself in the census, he was listed as café proprietor. The café—how wrong you are to think it was another dirty cave on Main Street—this café was his own house. Even a lesser Bothwick would have a well-built house with paneling and two oak stairways and a library that never had a book in it. His was now piled to the ceiling with cases of Schlitz.

On my yearly trips home I had occasionally driven by Dido's place and even sometimes caught her hanging clothes or carrying empty cases out to the garbage pails. I never stopped, and I don't think she recognized my half-wave. As I expected, she looked seedy and blotchy-faced. Alphonse, a few degrees less prejudiced than my mother, told me that she was often drunk by the time the children came home from school.

But I wanted to see for myself, and I had promised Mother to try to collect for our services to Norman. The same day last spring that Mother had told me about the bill, I drove over to the Bothwicks' and parked my car on what had been the lawn. The house had been set back off the street in a grove, and Norman had made a crescent drive so that you could park in front of the door. The crushed stone had all grown up in weeds. A ladder of signs promised cold beer, steak sandwiches, fish and chips, steamers, chicken, homemade pastries, but you knew you could only be sure of the beer.

All the original furniture in the house had been burned up or just fallen apart. The living room was filled with a crazy tangle of metal chairs, like the ones we used to have in the business, but cheaper, and little card tables. At one of them sat a long-haired child with a coloring book. She was filling in the last of a great purple turtle.

"Your mother?" I asked.

"Mom!" she shouted, beginning now on the orange feet.

Dido came out of the back and stared across the bar at me, squinting a little as if she wasn't going to recognize me.

"Whatya want? Hurry it up," she said.

"How've you been?" I asked.

"Looking for business?"

She did have spunk talking to me like that with the whole house falling apart and probably not a scrap of food in the refrigerator.

"I'll have a beer."

She poured it carefully. Her nails were dirty.

"I know it's five hundred. You tell Mame and Alphonse that I don't have it, and let him suck his lips on that. I should've let them keep the body for security. Or does it have to be somebody alive to satisfy you?"

A line from one of Alphonse's pamphlets almost came out: "We try to deal respectfully with the departed, to comfort and soothe the lot of the living."

"Now look, Dido, you don't think we'd put the squeeze on you—"

"Oh, no, you wait your turn, nervous as crows until it's easy to make the clean-up. When I was a kid, I used to hear that the Maigreys only owned two caskets and that after everybody'd left the cemetery, you went back, dumped the body into the hole, and took away the coffin."

Her daughter had done a nice job on the orange legs and now stared at us. This was evidently a new theme for her. It beats me how people are so fascinated with the death business, even children. Often I mention something about caskets at a party, and everything stops, not with horror or because it's in bad taste, but out of simple savage wonder.

"How do you want to take your cut? Would one white five-year-old child do? You could keep her for collateral until the insurance money comes in."

She grabbed the kid and threw her like a Yo-yo toward me, but I didn't reach out a hand. That's where Alphonse would have started stroking, and the kid would have screamed, but we all stood apart like animals waiting for the whip.

I wanted to say something honest and right to Dido, but

stared instead into the fireplace, full of empties and wadded newspapers. It had above it a lovely mantelpiece, oak with grape clusters and vines at either end. Some Bothwick had covered it with yellow varnish, and for once that was a good idea. It was the kind of fireplace you see in English inns, and it was the best thing in the room. People chucking beer bottles into the fireplace had chipped the Delft plaques at the side, but inside its yellow cocoon, the mantelpiece was secure. Back in Westmount, my fireplace had a marble top from a London flat that was bombed out. The antique dealer I bought it from told me that only one wall of the house stood, with four floors of fireplaces intact. Everyone in the building had been killed.

Dido shook her finger across the room at me. "No," she said, "this is one time you won't get your way. I remember how your mother conned us out of our dining room table when my father died. You're not getting a speck of dust out of this house."

Twenty years away from this town, I thought, and the only reaction to my name is the fear that I will steal their furniture and melt down their gold teeth. Dido and all the others couldn't be told that I had given up collecting beautiful old things when I learned their price. Somebody always has to die or sell out before you can grab their possessions away for a few dollars. And then what do you have but a few pieces of wood or glass or pewter that never will belong to you. Dido would not believe I had grown this wise. In order not to disappoint her image of me, I scowled my way out of her living room.

SOMEWHERE
BETWEEN THE
SKY AND THE
GROUND WE
TRY TO LIVE

❧ Even before dawn spread itself grudgingly down the olive groves of Delphi and over the smokestacks and tangled railroad tracks outside of Paris, three thousand miles west a white truck delivered two elaborately wrapped silver men to an elevator at the base of a tower. The men walked heavily the last few steps, waving conservatively to the few quiet witnesses. When the attendants had slid them onto the molded couches and bolted the hatch of their steel capsule, the cameras swung over the metal garden in which the silver men lay; in it grew spirals, cranes, spires, guide wires, all shadow and lace, extending upward like insect feelers. They lay waiting for the magic moment of dawn. While ten million people heard their hearts beat and their patient voices repeating commands and saw the plumed takeoff and the loose spirals over a diminished planet, they believed for a little while that life might change.

As the silver men swam through space, those who had died in the less wonderful days had to be buried. That was what they were doing with Bob Muldoon. While such miraculous events were happening in the sky, a knot of nervous wet-eyed mourners followed the casket toward the vestibule of Sts. Peter and Paul's. One of the men, reaching for a hand-kerchief to clear his nose and wipe his eyes before the trip to the cemetery, jostled the woman next to him.

"I'm sorry," he whispered. "My God. This is awful. The idea of Muldoon in the ground. Did you know him well?"

"Cousin," she said. "I'm his cousin Ellen."

"Oh," he said. "Sure. I remember. He was always talking about you. I'm Red Cummings. Dick, that is." Nobody had called him Dick for years, but he always began hopefully with strangers. "We used to be in the same firm. He's my first close friend to die. I can't believe it."

Mary Muldoon and the teen-aged children were spotted with enraged tears over their abandonment by the provident man. The steps of the church were steep, and for a moment or two it looked as if the red knuckles of the straining off-duty firemen, who were the paid bearers, might upset the white spray and let the casket fall, splinter, and, horrors, open upon Muldoon's powdered face, stirring his well-arranged hair, and tearing the rosary from his flattened fingers. The knot of people behind the firemen prayed that that would not happen more than they had prayed for Muldoon during the rapid Mass before. They had several worries to choose from: the delicate men alone in the sky, Muldoon, and, most of all, themselves.

All the friends and relatives had been treating themselves as invalids during the morning, getting in and out of cars thoughtfully, breathing carefully, staring at their hands and feet with some wonder, and finally jostling against the others, proving that firm flesh would respond. That was how Dick Cummings turned to Ellen Harvey and was relieved by her aliveness. For a second he thought of bold possibilities, like reaching out for her gloved hand, patting her shoulder, pressing his body against hers, whispering some words more comforting than air could transport. But they simply stood drawn together, glancing like frightened animals at each other, until the door of the hearse opened and the bearers, who had played their scaring game well, straightened up with sad smiles and melted into the following black station wagon.

"You have a ride." He made it into a statement of fact.

"No," she said. "I took a taxi to the church."

"Ride with me." Squaring his shoulders so that she would not take it seriously but only as a natural responsibility that he might assume, especially to the relative of a dead friend.

The procession was being hurried away to accommodate a wedding scheduled for eleven-thirty. The first guests were hovering inside or near their cars trying to shut their eyes to the hearse. The funeral director swooped his charges away from the curb so rapidly that by the time Dick Cummings had opened the door for her and briskly settled himself before the wheel, the last car had fastened itself to the speeding cortege and disappeared beyond the cop's agitated hand.

"My God, they're gone. Lost them. Do you know the way to the cemetery?"

"Yes," she said. "We'll have to hurry. The procession gets to go through lights and all. We'll have to fight traffic."

Which they did. Sitting in their best unfamiliar black in the Saturday morning sunlight in front of red lights, while sneakered women in pastel slacks with great heads of plastic curlers pushed their laundry carts across the windshield before them. They stared at a cautious old man in a green plaid car coat figuring whether the light would hold long enough for him to make it safely across. He dangled a foot daringly into the gutter, then picked it up and put it safely beside the other one.

They thought of the same thing at that moment. "Poor Muldoon," he said. "He didn't live to be that careful."

They studied the old man, who seemed to be tasting the air, trying to live forever in the ugliest shopping center along Northern Avenue. "It's terrible," she said. "Bob Muldoon isn't here any more. Two weeks ago, right outside that super-market I saw him putting the groceries in the trunk, and he got into the car and drove off, sitting just the way we are now." The small bones and the blue veins in her hands tight-ened. She thought she might cry again, and leaned strongly against the seat trying to stare the layers of neon signs and the enormous parking lots into some kind of reality.

When the light changed, he said: "We'll never get to the

cemetery. I don't think either of us wanted to anyway. My wife doesn't expect me right home. If I were alone, I'd go to a bar and have a drink. Would you? Or shall I take you back to where you came from?"

"I'll stay with you." The world outside was far too unsubstantial to be faced alone. Already she was dreading the moment that they would have to improvise some kind of goodbye. She seemed to spend a ridiculous amount of time getting ready to say good-bye to people. She knew after a certain point in life that good-byes occurred more often, but the knowledge never prepared for the fact.

Hours later, she might consider how she could have prevented the rest of the day. Said, "No thanks, I'm walking to the bus." Or, "Goodness, I wouldn't want to put you to the trouble. Just leave me off here." Or hidden behind work or sorrow or indifference. But the world terrified her that morning. Alone on the street, she would become like the unsure old man, testing the security of cement and stone. At least the car was a shell against the pressing world.

And in the middle of the day, with light falling on creaking floor boards usually covered by darkness, they entered a booth in the Lotus Tavern as if it were another pew. The little yellow lamps, never turned off, burned redundant over each table. Old dust hung in quiet patience where the sun fell.

They might have remained cautious before talk if the owner had not appeared, a messenger beside the booth. "Both guys are all right," he said. "The guys up in the capsule. They just talked with the President. You could hear them talking like they were right here. What'll you have, folks?"

They had whisky on the rocks and stared hard at the glasses. They were crouching on narrow shelves in their minds, unsure of what direction to spring, to make some awful summary or prophecy or to be clever or sympathetic.

We could, he thought, make a movie of our heads at work, getting ready to talk, to bury Muldoon, here as well as any place. And what would come to mind as obituary? A good kind man whom we never noticed. "To the men in the sky and all of us down here. And to Bob Muldoon."

"May we have as quiet a death as his," she said.

"Yes, we don't have to remember him shrinking into a mess in a hospital bed, half his body replaced with plastic and the other with decay. When I think about it, I hope it comes as a surprise to me too. I guess it doesn't do much good making plans about dying though. When I was eight, a kid in the same grade drowned and got buried in a white casket, and all of us marched to the church behind it. I thought then about dying all day long, how I would look and how that kid, a homely little thing he was, how he'd look as an angel and where they'd station him. One of the nuns figured out he might be at the school crossing watching over us. But some of the sentimental girls got hung up on the idea that he could just be in one of the cherub faces up behind the main altar. In a big wave of piety everybody volunteered for altar boy duty to see if he really was hung up there."

"Let's just hope we get to go back to some favorite place." She had a public voice with which she made transitions. The tone indicated that it was time to move on to another topic.

Muldoon had told him that Ellen worked for some nonprofit agency that gave out information about public affairs, that she lectured nights at the municipal university, and that she took herself a little too seriously. The family was at first disturbed by her sitting in libraries and laughing aloud about something in a book, but she managed herself in their old age well. Her aunts and uncles had with conspicuous effort left home in their mid-thirties by means of rectory weddings. They saw marriage, when they had occasion to look in its direction, as a mutual benefit association. There were indiscussable liabilities, but someone was always there at the right or left of you to correct your stories or supply the matches or mostly to be a wall, offering protection until the wall fell. Then you had the memory of it. Dick was a lawyer, and from the divorce cases he had seen, this was a fair estimate.

As he sat looking at Ellen, he realized that except for a certain nervousness, a kind of tidy caution, she could have been anyone's wife, and for all he knew, most mothers. In the middle years it comes to the same thing, those who marry and those who don't, he thought. No matter what, one goes out more lonely than one comes into the world.

Usually he did not snare anyone in great skeins of questions, but it seemed all right in this case to ask her where she spent summers, how Mary Muldoon would manage, what the chances for war might be.

Preferring this to the indirect research of sneaky inquiries, she answered him as directly as she knew. It was like having a listener who expected to be saved by what he heard. Or someone who had not heard words for a long time and was feeding off of them with hunger that could not have been faked. In the last few years she had quite often gathered together all the details of her life and discovered that they made a very small clump. By rearrangement she could offer anyone a satisfactory version. She realized that her life, small as it was, had now merged with history, and there it was, as much a biography as Cleopatra's or a thirteenth-century peasant's. And at the end, really, what difference? Therefore in talking about her life she had learned to use a flat tone appropriate to some minor and generally tedious event in history.

"You see," she was telling him, "all lives are really somewhat alike, if you can get up on a mountain and look down on them. But most of the time we are busy in the valley."

"You're quite right," he said. "Your life, mine, Muldoon's. What difference? If we only knew that before making the great struggle. I mean, think of the days we tear ourselves apart. And for what? If you kept looking at yourself from the perspective of maybe a hundred years you wouldn't."

"We can't do that, of course. That's the point. We're temporal because we're mortal."

"I wonder. Do some people, not just Carmelites or convicts on two-hundred-year sentences, live outside of time?"

The line between sentimentality and truth is so thin and stretches so many different ways that she realized that grand statements and fancy reflections are embarrassing necessities. Dick Cummings, running off at the mouth now, was still entirely sincere. She too was engulfed by loose emotions on occasion. Recently her own tears had surprised her. Passing the television set on the way to the kitchen to wash her dinner plate, she had seen a crowd of Belgians standing in the rain at the entrance to a mine which had crushed twenty of their relatives. The women leaning against a rope which kept them from the mouth of the mine were waiting to be told what the commentator had already let his audience know. The mine superintendent in a trenchcoat took up the megaphone to tell the straining women that the bodies had been found. Ellen's eyes filled with tears. How could one comfort the chunky and agonized woman in the center of the screen who had not kissed him good-bye, had not held his hand, or stroked his back, except in the most mechanical way, for years. No one could tell this woman how the ache would diminish from its beginning in scraped-out misery when a hand could hardly raise itself or an eye focus on part of the world until ten years from now she might at the end of a back-breaking day look at the photograph on the dresser and not be able to see it at all. Ellen believed that on the whole it was an age of private crying. For standing in your own closet or cell and crying alone. And then, putting cold towels on your swollen eyes, swallowing a few tranquilizers, and coming out smiling. Ellen would not have been surprised at all if Dick Cummings cried, away from the sight of his wife and children.

"Even the schools," he said, "train children to live for the minute, and when they graduate they realize that the minute is in the past. Every day I realize how badly educated I was. The old folks put me through the Christian Brothers and a year in the novitiate. I came out and then took the rest of college at St. Ulric's. It wasn't even as good as high school in those days. And sometimes I think it is a wonder any of us turned out well, or if not well, we're not in jails or madhouses. No, we're just dying instead."

They could see out the windows of the bar to the street, where fathers were patiently pushing children in thick parkas toward a morning in Woolworth's or the Top Value Drugstore. These thickening men with cigarette coughs followed the memory of a father or uncle who thirty years before had called out the same cautions, threats, and offers and who had slouched through dutiful weekends, only sure that the children would repeat the process years from then. All the futile little kindnesses paraded by.

"I wish," she said, "we did not even destroy the snow."

"There must be places in the world where they do not."

"I doubt that. We've gotten too good at destruction for that."

"In the war . . ." he began and stopped.

"What about in the war?"

"Oh, nothing. I hate guys that drag the war around like a pull toy. But at one time in the war, I was in an evergreen forest, big black trunks, and black-green needles except when the sun fell for about an hour around noon and shimmered them brown and dry. It was the full of the moon and sometimes in the perfect whiteness at night I thought I was dead too."

"Were you afraid?"

He had just been thinking about that when she asked. "No. Not a bit. It seemed the most natural thing in the world to die there. We didn't go to the point of suicide or being careless to prove how easy it was. At least, I don't think anyone did."

In his head grew this frantic scheme. How would it be to drive out of here, leaving behind the decaying speckled drifts, and speed along gritty throughways northward, up mountain roads, toward the dark-green forest, the needles still clasping a handful of the first snowfall? The roads would narrow and finally on a logging trail, only two slight depressions on the floor of the forest, they would be absolutely alone, the first to come since the snow. Relentlessly his mind stripped away all excess—their age, work, obsessions, tics, habits. He arranged the dream until they stood under the straightest, greenest tree. If only by holding head to head, hand to hand, they could get beyond conversation, say everything without saying it, get over the nervous preliminaries. That, he thought, is why people rush to bed. And if I did not know just enough to distrust it, I would try again.

Silence tensed her bones. But then, why talk? Predictable conversation lay before them in programmed dialogue. She could introduce a list of his St. Ulric's classmates, and they could reflect upon how stupid, successful, insecure, hearty, well or poorly married, dead or alive, each might be. They could use up the next hour, wear out their tongues, and then say good-bye, disappearing under the scurrying and rustling words. Muldoon, the subject of such frenzied attention the last three days, was best let alone. Dick's family would presumably lead to rash confidences and Kodacolor children's pictures. If she had known exactly how, she would have drawn from his skull the real week in the wartime forest, but she knew his talk would always get in the way of the picture.

The major tragedy of middle age is, she thought, the reluctance to begin again with people. In the church vestibule I should not have leaned toward him. In a minute now, when he faces the end of the drink and announces the next stage, I will be prepared.

"Lunch," he said, as she had guessed. "We've got to eat. Poor Muldoon, we didn't say much about him. Well, he probably wouldn't have cared."

She was thinking of the burial dinners on the big stone tables in the catacombs near the freshly filled shelf and the vases for shed tears, around which the mourners made the same kind of conversation.

"Do you know any place around here?" He asked with a shrinking look which she interpreted as general guilt, which he was fighting by telling himself that if she had been another man, they would have gone to lunch without thinking about it.

She was bolder than in her head's practicing. "Come with me, back to my house. There must be something in the refrigerator."

"Oh, fine." The decision sat between them in the car and prevented their looking directly at each other.

Her house was the result of nine moves. It was both perilous and permanent. It was the last house in a row of sturdy three-story miniature castles, built on a bluff around 1890 for their occupants' retirement. It looked down at the suffering river flowing toward the bay. On the river's edge great gas and oil silos sat amid smoky piles of refuse—tires, mattresses, plastic raincoats, stale food—she never discovered what. The untended piles never burned down completely, although no one seemed to replenish them. Their gritty plumes were part of the skyline as much as the shabby gulls and the back sides of sturdy little businesses that appeared to have no front entrances—Fezulo's Noodle Corp., Sue-Ann's Findings, Stanley's Body Works, and, nearest the edge of the river, the Swan Laundret, a green-and-white shrine open round the clock presided over by a Chloroxed family of cheerless robots, their hands shriveled into permanent white ridges, their blue eyes staring reproachfully at the mountains of repetitious stain and predictable grease spots.

Against the sky on one side, the house looked taller than it really was. Anyone their age might have had grandparents who once lived in such a big barn and could afford benevolent feelings toward it—not the house of childhood traumas, but a holiday house, where truces were held, where suspension of hostilities permitted excess, to be paid for later when you returned to your parents' orderly living rooms: "Must you show off, you little devil?" "How many times do we have to tell you to behave?" "We were mortified, absolutely mortified, and before Grandma too . . ."

As she predicted he said: "Why, look at that ark of a place. You own all of it? It's great."

They parked in the cinder driveway, beside an absurdly old and dented car. "I rent the top floor," she explained, "to three Chinese engineering students. Word must go out to Taiwan for identical replacements because when they leave, their duplicates arrive. I hate whispering and distant talk in a language I know. The Chinese comes through the walls like dogs barking or snow tires on the expressway. It is comforting and asks nothing. The cooking smells are good, and when they laugh a lot, I don't have to figure out what's funny. You don't have to worry about their social life. Whatever it is, it arrives all made up like paper flowers or folded cranes. And, besides, I look upon them as the advance guard. When the final invasion comes, I have had advanced experience. I've lived with them, see?"

He wished that she did not have to be so brittle, but supposed it was turned on, generally as self-protection. Should one blame porcupines or skunks?

He waited until he was safely inside the solid front door and taking his rubbers off at the combined boot chair, coat rack, mirror, and hat stand to tell her how much he liked the house. He had been a child in a bungalow with little dark rooms and married into a ranch house with small bright rooms like a department store window. The dimensions of Ellen's house allowed colossal mistakes which here turned into successes: a gold room collected by her mother simply for admiration, an uncurtained sun parlor with a window seat and sagging wicker chairs, a wide stairway that made a secret of where it went, and a study as he imagined it should be with two cluttered desks and several hanging photographs in thin black frames—Ellen as a bridesmaid, Ellen on a camel in front of the Sphinx, a candid of her snapped during the last summer when she was lecturing a Golden Agers group, all the old people nodding or waiting for lunch, their varicose-veined legs largely spread before them, their butts falling over the edges of the folding chairs.

"I must," he said reluctantly, "call my wife."

She was getting ready to close him into the study with the telephone when he told her: "Don't leave. Stay. I won't be a minute." Telephoning is a lonely business, too perilous to be managed without support, especially when one is trying to ransom an afternoon.

"Look, I won't be home for lunch. I'm sorry, but I ran into some people. Oh, yes, it was a terribly sad funeral. No, Mary held up well. Should I get anything on the way back? All right. See you later."

His wife had seemed surprised that he had bothered to call. He would have liked to have shocked her into recognizing his value by telling her where he was, but he had not really figured out where he was even then. Ellen stood at the window, trying to stare at the flat river up which a white oil tanker drifted. But, instead, she was seeing a cutaway of his ranch house, mobs of Saturday children strewn around the living room, his pert wife on the kitchen extension, angry at his defection. He really shouldn't have stayed, Ellen thought, he should have been sent home. This lunch was a luxury neither of us could afford. But remembering Muldoon again, she considered that no self-indulgence invented could make up for dying.

What visitors came to her house were usually in clumps. To concentrate on a single individual was very difficult and especially on one so greedy of her past and present. This middle-aged child reached out to touch the books and stare at the photographs as if he expected to graft himself into the place. Next he would be opening the bureau drawers and making an inventory of the pantry shelves. Not that she wasn't flattered; such close scrutiny can turn the head entirely around.

He pulled a book from a shelf. "Do you know how hard it is for me to read a book all the way through. I suppose concentration is a problem for you as much as for me, but the way we all live makes it impossible to give yourself— Oh, I suppose you think I've had too much to drink the way I'm going on." He sat down, discouraged by the poverty of his revelations, wishing that they might skip over the next few weeks of talk.

"I will find some lunch." And she left as if to hunt it in some thicket or dip a net into the cove.

Hearing the distant clattering, he dared to move toward her desk and to sit in the chair behind it. While we eat, he thought, I will tell her about myself as accurately as I can. He thought of making a list. One of the senior partners in his firm came to the office once or twice a month bearing in his yellow shaky hands a list of topics he wanted to gossip about.

So—the subheadings of his life, as they occurred to him:

Sleep: heavy. He supposed it to be motionless, trying to remember the next morning in what position he had fallen asleep. As a boy he had awakened slowly like a sunflower lifting, but at the last stage resurrected crisply new he faced days brighter and longer than any crafted before. Now he sprang toward his slippers, guilty of the wasted hours, wearing in his head a tired ache as if someone had hit him with a rubber mallet all night.

Dreams: few remembered, but the sense of their having

recently vacated, like tree branches bending after a speeding car has disappeared around the next corner. What exactly had happened in them attracted but frightened him. A few weeks ago, perhaps twice in a dream he had confidently swung into a familiar door—a drug store, a courtroom, a friend's house, his old office—grasped the knob, pulled it, and froze before the terrible sight of a burned-out shell. A gray man, his face looking the other way, spoke from the other side of the charred cavity: "Perhaps the only way to say the right thing, the absolutely right thing, is by saying nothing at all. Only thinking is required." What did it mean? It was like a scene from a foreign movie, the sort he had taken his wife to a couple of times and had been intensely disturbed by.

Wife: a good and tidy dull woman, who finished doing the dishes two seconds after the last person finished eating, who suffered children, house, pets, neighbors, holidays, vacations, an evening at the movies, as if they were minor sicknesses, as opposed to the major illness which was daily living. Her cheerfulness was tragic. Her worries were transparent. She was hurrying the years along as fast as possible, collecting news of diminished contemporaries leaning toward death and disease or misery. "I met George Desmond in the bank and he looked like death. What a change came over him! And he's exactly the same age as you." She talked in gusts. On most topics outside the family and other peoples' health, she was silent. But upon the introduction of references to their children, she sprang to life and could lecture in double time for several hours. At a party recently he watched the wife of the senior partner mention one of the children and then brace herself for the torrent. He seldom looked at her any more and realized that she had not made an interesting statement for several years. Most of the time he forgot about her and assumed that theirs was a perfectly safe marriage.

Children: now almost as unnoticed as the wife. At five years of age they had fallen out of love with him, and like former lovers regarded him with traces of embarrassment and distrust. Sometimes for a few days or a single hour he thought they had discovered him again. But their moods, like swallows, dipped and sped away. They had just been between flirtations. Not that he had expected them to be fascinated by him. In a way it was less trouble that they should be so indifferent. They could be bought free of some of their problems by money. The others they would try to marry out of and be surprised to find a new accumulation.

Work: like most jobs long and carefully done, dull. Clients, a selfish and spoiled bunch, more passionate about money than family or friends. Judges, a senile tribe of former back-slappers who had been told black robes looked well on them, and who according to whim or the taste of their morning coffee decided right or left. Law libraries, fine rooms burdened with incidents of greed, chronicles of procrastination and indifference, pointless reversals, the slow fencing-in of individual rights, the endless searching for exception or precedent, a game nobody could win. Best parts of work: arriving in the morning washed in the faith that today might be different and leaving in the afternoon.

Miscellaneous: this was everything and nothing. God, for

one. In shadow a good deal of the time. Just when He might emerge, the homily every Sunday drove Him back. The Good Citizen God of the homily was increasingly involved in fair play. "Those who tire easily do not win; winners do not tire. With training, you can cross the final goal line to salvation, in your hands clasping the ball. The ball, dear friends, is your immortal soul." The child beside him in the pew blew his nose, the man in front of him shifted with alarm or a nervous twitch. And yet it was an index of smallness to be troubled by a homily. There had to be shape imposed on the days. Did nothing more than respect for the past draw them here of a Sunday? What dark fears secured them in terror? What message did they expect from the clouds or sea or themselves? He had once long ago believed in order and even more in a suspended state of invisible rightness. He had struggled toward both during the climbing years. Such heights made his head ache now. If he did not remember his nighttime dreams, he was more aware of the daytime ones, visiting and revisiting familiar ones. A particular favorite was the snowy forest, another was gulls sweeping the sky, another was the sea itself. There were no people in any of these: they would have had to stand outside the frame, looking in upon the perfection. It was not that Dick Cummings was a nature-lover. He had never dragged the family through the national parks or on boating trips. He knew instinctively that most beauty is best thought about and not seen.

Meanwhile, she was trying to be purposeful in the kitchen, tinkering with the stove, careening into the refrigerator, scraping her ingenuity for a domestic success, dreaming her way into tomorrow. She could never enjoy the present, to be totally there; her vision swiveled to the past or toward the future. When she was alone, this was no inconvenience, but voices asked: "Do you think I should go home for Christmas?" "How stable is the regime in Cambodia?" "Should we buy paper clips from Poland?" She was a fixture at high school assemblies and Rotary luncheons and Women's Club Guest Nights. What appealed to her in the squirrel cage of talking was that all the words were lost immediately. When the compliments faded, the floral centerpiece was seized by the chairman, and they had already blessedly forgotten her name, her message, her face, their presence. It was a study in oblivion. Most people and incidents are easily forgotten. And if remembered, for all the wrong reasons.

She carried the plates into the dining room, experimenting with them in various places at the table, until the food was probably cold. Then she called him into the room.

"Say, this room is beautiful," and then he bent his head humbly at words that seemed like strange-shaped rocks falling from his lips. "What I mean is, when I was a boy, I had a jigsaw puzzle somebody gave me when I had the measles or something, a beautiful puzzle with a wooden back, and the picture—why it was like this room." She looked around, discovering the room again. It had a series of windows, bowing away from the house, beneath them a window seat with a tufted blue cushion, faded into frosted gray-blue. Quantities of sun had bleached the room; the sun had fallen through the glass curtains so long that even at night or on dark days or with the shutters pulled out of the wall, the gold still fell on the Chinese carpet and toward the decanters and the silver service. The room was a memorial, he thought, to a past perhaps no one had experienced.

"It has been a good room to eat in," she said, trying not to claim too much. "Actually, I don't eat as much as sit here and think."

"I know why," he said. "It's the happiest room I have ever been in. We see so few lovely things these days that we have lost the language to define them."

What he was thinking was—if they could only be sealed off forever in this room. At this point in their lives, not to live, but to die. What an odd thought. He was no suicidal type. Lacked the reasons that pushed the tortured young or old over the sides of buildings or into ponds at midnight. Partially afraid and thinking he might miss something. Without warning, for instance, in the vestibule of a church this woman had appeared. With all her disguises off in this shelter she was more tender and vulnerable than any creature alive. He stared a long time at her, amused by the possibility that he might announce that he had fallen in love with her, and at that moment the sides of the room, even the sea beyond, would fall away as a skillfully painted backdrop, and the lights would come on to show an auditorium of jeering move-goers, tilting their heads back and stamping their feet with pleasure. We are not that funny, he protested. We are, of course, not tragic. We put ourselves here and are not frozen. We are simply eating a meal, and all we want to do is to avoid death.

My God, how pompous I become, he thought. It is only lunch. But as he looked at her carefully laying the knife and fork across the plate, and stared into the hollow of her neck beneath the sharp chin, he was taken again. She was complete, entire, waiting now for old age and death. Whole. Waiting for the roller coaster to plunge down the slope to the tunnel. Held unbreathing at the top of the Ferris wheel for a second, heart frozen, eye catching the absolute whole of the unreal little world beneath. Inside their bodies they would remember flight as well as death. Muldoon again became the third guest at the table.

"Even if one makes all the right preparations for immortality, they get wiped away with a wet rag the morning of death. Now you, for instance." He waved to include the house. "I would be so grateful if I had lived your life. Isn't that a funny thing to say?"

"I wish," she said, "you wouldn't worry so much about what I think about your statements. Why do you do that?"

"I suppose because I'm trying to look at the scene through your eyes. I know how sentimental and cheap I must seem. The longer we live and the more cracked the lips become and the shorter the breath, the less daring our sentences. Twenty years ago I would have been able to talk with you, really talk, but I suppose I wouldn't have had anything to say."

"We should probably give up on words. They keep diminishing us." She made the one right gesture out of several thousand unattempted. She reached across the table and took his hand. "The world is a very perilous place, both in the way one comes in and goes out and the chanciness of both events. And one of the most frightening motions is lifting the edges of the mask before a stranger."

"Or crying," he said. "One night in that forest I told you about, I cried. For the beauty. This morning I was on the edge when I touched your shoulder. For misery and my own growing old. And now again here out of deep happiness." The bones of his hand caught hers in a steel net. "I feel as if you had pulled me back from dying."

"I am an ordinary woman who can scarcely save myself. I have little energy left for anything else, except for trying not to be noticeably insane—to myself. What the others think is irrelevant. But if you are endangered by madness there is a particular tension which you grow to dread. After many attempts to take you over, it stops. It halts in some crevice or other, blinking its little eyes, darting out its hungry tongue, knowing it will starve. The idea that I can comfort anyone else has never presented itself."

"Not the people you work with?"

"They're like the people you work with, decent more of the time than you expect them to be, once or twice a year letting themselves become human, after suffering some disaster or other. The inside, greater horrors, are always untended. They give up interesting each other ever again, no matter how major the sicknesses the hypochondriacs devise, no matter how tragic the stories of the self-pitying are. Unfortunately, they have become objects, and not very successful ones."

They had stretched arms across the table. They could have been swimming and reaching for each other's hands, but it was also as if they were offering their whole selves inside the caged hand.

"I have to tell you how lonely I have been," he said. "But

you might laugh. Me lonely with a whole houseful of men
and women related to me. When I try to talk, though, it's as
if I had interrupted a lifelong conversation. The children actually practice patience with me, an occasional be-kind-to-the
old-fool night. This morning I was thinking my mouth is open
all the time, all day, and I never get a chance to say what I
think. Now I come here, and I don't have to tell you anything."

Afternoon filled the room, which was at its best in the
morning or at night, with drawn curtains. If there was anything good in the house he must have it. She pushed back her
chair. "Let's look at the river for a bit. Leave the dishes."

If you sat on the davenport at the back of the room, as he
did, you saw only gulls and the flat water as if Fezulo's Noodle
Corp. and the Swan Laundret had not yet been thought of.
You did not see that the edges of the bay were crusted with
what might be detergent or ice; the sky matched the center
of the bay so well that they melted into each other. Through
the ceiling the Chinese engineering students were leaving
jabs of sentences to drift, each beginning at the same ex-
cited, happy pitch and going nowhere. Once in a while the
sentences were jointed with laughter.

She brought two glasses of Scotch gravely to the edge of
the great red carpet, handed him one, and stood uncertainly.

"Here," he said, drawing her to sit close to him. "Do you
ever wish that you had been marked to be extraordinary?
That you could build out of shadows any shape you wanted
and take off without leaving a note for a rain forest or New
Orleans or nowhere in particular. Or suppose that you wanted
to run across country, over lawns, down afternoon streets,

panting through red lights, racing the buses, puffing up the inclines, skidding a little in the graveled gutter, scudding along under the maples—maybe in spring when the keys are falling. My God, how lovely! You know, just once at St. Ulric's I was on the cross-country team. I was no athlete. But I just liked long-distance running. And it was spring and I was out in trunks and skivvy slogging along, entirely happy, and a car crawled by, slowly enough so I could hear through the open window the man say to his kids: 'Look at that damn fool. Look at that nut now, will you.'

"I went on running, of course, but thinking about the fat man in the car. And I still remember the way he looked at me. If I had been extraordinary, it wouldn't have mattered, would it?"

"When I think," she said, "of how much energy we spend not to be noticed, while on the other hand we hope someone is calling to us. And the madness of the pendulum, one day noticing and the other day rejecting the call. And the other person not knowing when we are going to heed and only daring to call a limited number of times. When we make up our minds to answer, the other person has stopped calling. It's enough to make you wish people were programmed. Except that all the misery and joy and interest in human beings comes from their never being sure about the inside of the other's skull."

.　　　.　　　.

Above them the sincere efficient astronauts who had almost no secrets whirled and tumbled, their body wastes collected to be weighed, their blood and brain charted, reported to great consoles manned by white-coated scientists, their breath whispering through radio waves into a stranger's ear, their steady dependable hearts beating on national TV into thirty million sets. Their neat cheerful wives smiled, waved, patted the children's heads, and made waffles, while their husbands tumbled and spun in their public eggshell. Beneath the watchers wished them well, frightened by their poise and ease.

•　　　　•　　　　•

"Do you suppose they've come down yet?" Dick Cummings asked. Somewhere south on the same ocean of which this bay was a part the capsule might be bobbing perilous on a cushion of thousands of feet of cold green sea in which strong fish swam and far below blind things spread themselves this way and that a few inches an hour. "No," he said, "don't turn on the television. It might somehow not give them luck, the poor men."

"What a funny thing to call them," she said, "with the rest of the nation envying. But I understand. If you look at the sky too long, you might find it hard to focus on what's below."

What she was saying to him through the fading afternoon was that they had already said good-bye in her mind; she was gathering the rooms into a smaller space and trying to cover the emptiness of his going. This too, she thought, is a habit of middle age, fearing to enjoy anything because you will miss it later, not allowing yourself an indulgence that will become an expensive habit.

"It would be just as well, falling in love with the sky in the long run. I suppose," he said, "you know that I've fallen in love with you, or think I'm on the edge of it, me—a few thousand mornings away from Bob Muldoon. No good could come of it."

"I suppose not. We had better stop at the beginning," she said, having studied sensibleness so long that she settled automatically into it.

He was explaining to himself patiently. "I can't stay, and I'd make life hell if I went and came. Neither of us could stand it. The more I came, the longer it would take to leave every time. The more I'd have to run out at night and call you from a telephone booth beside the freeway or outside a garage, and with the noise of all the pumps running and tires thudding, I'd stand in the neon light and beg to come over here. Or we'd drive to a motel a hundred miles away that had stained furniture and dirty bedspreads and dead mice in the closets, and I'd wake up in the night sure that someone had recognized the car. That could kill both of us."

"Yes," she said, "when you leave today, you must really go away." She lived so much in remembering that she was seeing today in a frame five or ten years from now. Knowing how inevitably life lives itself, she was hurrying him away. She had seen the old tear open Christmas gifts the minute they received them and then settle back in their wheelchairs asking: "Well, what's the next holiday? When's my birthday?" Looking at him carefully, she saw the earliest marks of death, knew how he would slump double on a gray sidewalk or trying to concentrate on the intern's hand while he gave the last injection. And she, pudgy-faced and nearsighted, would read the next day's obituary notice and perhaps stand in the damp church vestibule watching the casket jerk crazily down into the waiting hearse.

"I am really going to try to leave you. I am really going to try," he said and grabbed her shoulders tensely before he let himself out the front door. He did not look back to the house as he drove away.

She sat a long time in the room watching the shadows dim its edges. Then it was time for the evening news, for the avuncular prophet to tell all the world's aches. When she had been a child, the radio voice had distributed gifts and birthday presents. Tonight, before recounting the day's little miseries, the newscaster began happily to trace the plucky course of the good, glad, lucky astronauts from the morning launch to the slow curved landing on the great sea cushion. Lifted in the harness out of the silver bell and set in the cleared circle of the great deck pressed round with cheering sailors, they lurched gingerly across the deck. "Wow," one of them said to the microphone suddenly under his chin. "It's tremendous out there. I can't wait to see the photographs." On some air force base the camera found one of the smiling wives: "Oh, I wasn't worried a second. No, the only thing I worried about was whether I'd get my wash done. No, it was a perfectly ordinary day around here."

A NOTE ON THE TYPE

The text of this book is set in Electra, a typeface designed by W(illiam) A(ddison) Dwiggins for the Mergenthaler Linotype Company and first made available in 1935. Electra cannot be classified as either "modern" or "old style." It is not based on any historical model, and hence does not echo any particular period or style of type design. It avoids the extreme contrast between "thick" and "thin" elements that marks most modern faces, and is without eccentricities which catch the eye and interfere with reading. In general, Electra is a simple, readable typeface which attempts to give a feeling of fluidity, power, and speed. This book was composed, printed, and bound by The Colonial Press Inc., Clinton, Massachusetts. Typography and binding design by Bonnie Spiegel.